COLLECTION

A CENTURY OF AMERICAN DREAMS

DALLAS SCHULZE

USA TODAY BESTSELLING AUTHOR

SATURDAY'S CHILD

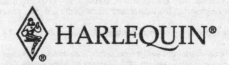

HARLEQUIN®

TORONTO • NEW YORK • LONDON
AMSTERDAM • PARIS • SYDNEY • HAMBURG
STOCKHOLM • ATHENS • TOKYO • MILAN • MADRID
PRAGUE • WARSAW • BUDAPEST • AUCKLAND

To my husband, Art,
who cooked and cleaned and sympathized.

ISBN 0-373-51283-X

SATURDAY'S CHILD

This edition published by arrangement with Harlequin Books S.A.

® and TM are trademarks of the publisher. Trademarks indicated with ® are registered in the United States Patent and Trademark Office, the Canadian Trade Marks Office and in other countries.

Visit us at www.eHarlequin.com

Printed in U.S.A.

Chapter One

Lying in bed, Katie McBride stared up at the dark ceiling, waiting. She'd been waiting for over an hour now, listening to every creak of the stairs, every closing of a door.

The church bells had long since tolled the hour of midnight. In respectable neighborhoods, respectable people were abed, sleeping peacefully in anticipation of waking the next morning to take up their respectable lives.

There were many words that could be applied to San Francisco's Barbary Coast but respectable was not one of them. The hours of darkness were peak business hours for the area's gambling halls, saloons and bordellos. The Barbary Coast never slept. An hour's sleep would cost an hour's profit—and profit was the one essential.

Profit was not on Katie's mind, though money was seldom far from it. But for Katie, money wasn't profit. It was survival. Survival and maybe, someday, a way out. Out of this shabby room in an even shabbier building; out of this tumbledown neighborhood that bordered on neighborhoods even more worn and tattered.

She'd spent most of her life in rooms much like this one. Her parents' finances had dictated their living conditions and their finances had fluctuated with all the regularity of the ocean's tide. If the show was going well and the theater was filled most nights, then they dined on oysters, roast beef and champagne. When the crowds were thin, they counted themselves lucky to have food at all.

Katie had spent all her nineteen years moving from place to place, never sure where the next meal was coming from or if there was going to *be* a next meal. Sean and Maggie McBride had come from Ireland, determined to make a new and better life for themselves in a fresh new land.

The theater was in their blood and they'd been sure that, in America, the footlights would shine brighter than they had in Ireland, the applause would be louder and every opening would herald a new success.

They'd brought their infant son with them, and a few years later, Katie had been born during a brief stop in Cleveland. The McBrides had dreamed of founding a new theatrical dynasty, like the Booths of years past and the Drews and Barrymores of more recent times. The name McBride would come to mean the finest in theater, the plays everyone wanted to see.

Katie rolled over in bed, staring at a patch of peeling wallpaper. Odd, how she'd given so little thought to her parents' dreams and aspirations when they'd been alive. It was only now that they were dead that she wondered if it had bothered them that Ibsen and

Shakespeare had given way to vaudeville. If it had, they'd never let it show.

Katie had been on the stage before she could walk, a living prop for a play whose title even her parents had forgotten by the time she was five. She'd danced and sung in theaters from Boston to Los Angeles. Once she'd even had a role in a Broadway play with Ethel Barrymore.

The McBride family had seldom been in one place for more than a few months at a time. Her parents had always believed that a great hit awaited them in the next town, the next theater, just around the next bend in the road. Katie had grown up to the sound of applause, the clicking of wheels on the railroad track and the smell of greasepaint.

In a way, this dingy room was the closest thing to a home she'd ever known. Certainly she'd lived here longer than she'd ever lived anywhere else. Her older brother, Colin, had left the McBride family act almost three years ago, tired of the endless wandering. Liking San Francisco best of all the endless succession of cities they'd traveled through, he'd settled there.

Katie had stayed with her parents, of course, until their death eight months earlier in New York City. They'd been crossing the street in front of their hotel when an automobile careened around the corner at a speed far in excess of that demanded by safety— nearly thirty miles an hour, one witness had guessed.

The impact had killed them both and Katie was suddenly an orphan. But not quite alone in the world. Colin had sent for her and she'd come all the way across the country to join him.

On the journey, she'd tried not to hope for too

much. Colin had said little enough in his few letters, which had often taken months to reach his family. Katie knew nothing of his life. Still, she'd allowed herself to dream—just a little.

A small house maybe—nothing fancy—just a cottage where she'd perhaps be able to grow a rose or two. They'd rented a house one summer in Connecticut and she'd never forgotten the scent of the roses that grew over the porch. She'd learn to cook and to clean and take care of Colin and for the first time in her life, she'd have a home.

But there was no cottage. No plot of ground to garden. There was just this one room, with a bathroom down the hall and one window that looked out on a street lined with shabby buildings inhabited by shabby people.

She didn't blame Colin that reality had fallen short of her dreams. In her nineteen years Katie had learned that life rarely did anything else. And prosperity was not as easily found as Mr. McKinley's political slogan had implied. A "full lunch pail" was still a dream for a large segment of the population. One could hardly blame Mr. McKinley of course, cut down in the prime of life as he had been. Most seemed to agree that Mr. Roosevelt had done a good job—hadn't he been elected in his own right, just last year?

Still, there was little enough work to be had, even for a strong-bodied man who was willing to work. Labor on the docks did not pay enough to live on and turned young men into old men before their time. Colin had done a bit of that and he'd worked as a clerk in a drugstore for a time. He'd been getting by, spend-

ing money as he made it, for he'd not been expecting
to have someone depending on him.

When Katie arrived, he'd taken a job as a dealer in
a saloon on the Barbary Coast. It was no job for a man
of his talents, and Katie had told him so, but it put
food on the table. It hadn't taken her long to see the
necessity of finding work herself. She could, perhaps,
have gone back to the theater. There were those who'd
remember her parents and be willing to help her in
their memory. Heaven knows, they'd always been
willing enough to help anyone who crossed their path.

But her future didn't lie in the theater. Though she'd
liked it well enough as a child, the excitement had
long ago worn off. She was tired of the tawdry trap-
pings and the only certainty in life being uncertainty.
She wanted a home and a family, a place to put down
roots.

She turned over and stared at the ceiling again.
Nearly three o'clock in the morning and Colin still
wasn't home. Not that he hadn't worked this late before, but it never failed to worry her. He'd laughed at
her fears, telling her that she wasn't to be worrying
about him. But she'd read the stories of men being
knocked over the head and shanghaied onto a ship in
the harbor. Colin was all she had left in the world. She
couldn't help but worry.

Still, he'd be furious if he knew she'd been lying
awake, waiting for him to come home. She closed her
eyes, willing herself to relax. If she didn't get rest,
she'd be falling asleep over her stitching work tomorrow. She had to believe that Colin could take care of
himself.

But what if something had happened to him?

Her eyes flew open and she stared up at the darkened ceiling, waiting, listening.

THE CROWD at the Rearing Stallion was reaching its nightly peak. Customers filled every table, drinking, gambling and spending their money. The midnight show had been a rousing success. Lily and her girls had shown a scandalous amount of shapely leg and sang songs that would have brought a blush to a maiden's cheek, were a maiden so foolish as to venture into the smoky room.

But the women who frequented the Rearing Stallion would have been hard-pressed to recall just when they'd lost their claim to that title. The brilliant silks and satins of their gowns glittered in the light of the newly installed electric chandeliers. They moved amongst the more somberly clad men like colorful birds in summer's brightest plumage.

The huge glass mirror that backed the bar reflected the crowd, making it seem twice as large. A wide mahogany staircase swept up along one papered wall, leading to the second floor, where rooms could be had for business requiring more privacy than the tables on the floor. Private card games as well as more romantic meetings made the second floor almost as profitable as the first.

Colin McBride paid no attention to the glittering swirl of people. When he'd first come to work at the Rearing Stallion, he'd been impressed by the sparkle of lights, the richly flocked walls and the warm gleam of wood. But it hadn't taken him long to see that it was only a facade.

In daylight, it was easy to see the dirt that marked

the walls, the scars in the wood where too many feet had scuffed over the floors, too many glasses had been slapped down on the bar. There was a crack across one corner of the huge mirror behind the bar. At night, a fancy feathered fan covered the crack, but during the day no one bothered with trying to hide it. The Rearing Stallion, in all its tawdry glory, was nothing more than a thin facade over a flaking background.

Colin didn't mind. After spending most of his life in the theater, he understood facades. Most things in life weren't entirely what they seemed and most people had one face they showed to the world and another face entirely that they wore in private.

There was no clock in the Rearing Stallion, nothing to remind the patrons of the hour, but Colin knew it must be nearing three. Three o'clock, and the game had been going on since ten. There was a small crowd gathered around the table, sensing the tension.

He dealt another round of cards, his face impassive. The game couldn't last much longer. Of the five players who had started, three had dropped out, their money gone. For the past two hours, it had been just two men facing each other across the table. But it couldn't last much longer.

"Damn you, Quentin." Joseph Landers threw down his hand in disgust when his opponent displayed four queens.

"Careful, Joseph. A gentleman always loses gracefully." Colin watched as the winner scooped the pile of money from the center of the table.

He knew Joseph Landers, by reputation at least. And the reputation wasn't good. The man was related by marriage to the Sterlings, one of San Francisco's

wealthiest families. No one knew for sure where his
money came from, but he always had enough to gamble. He was a poor loser and Colin had no doubt he'd
be a cheat also, if given the chance.

The other player was new to the Rearing Stallion,
or at least new to Colin. He was a tall man with thick,
dark-gold hair that would probably look much lighter
in the sunlight. Strong features and eyes of a startling
shade of blue, explained several of the ladies who
stood nearby, their attention more on the players than
on the game.

Colin dealt another hand, sensing that this would be
the final one. Landers had little enough left to gamble
and he'd get no credit at the Rearing Stallion.

The hand was played out with cruel speed. Landers
asked for two cards, which Colin dealt him silently.
After a moment, the stranger requested a single card,
his expression unchanging as he accepted it and
slipped it into his hand. Colin had already seen the
light flare in Landers's eyes as he arranged his own
cards. He shoved the last of his money into the center
of the table, the slightest tremor shaking his hands.
The stranger arched one eyebrow but silently matched
the bet.

Landers placed his cards on the table with a tri-
umphant flourish, a grin breaking over his thin features. A full house, aces and eights lay on the green
felt. He reached for the pot, sure of his triumph.

"You're always in such a hurry, Joseph." At his
opponent's quiet words Landers's hands froze over the
money. The other man spread his cards on the table
and Colin had to choke back a laugh. A royal flush
seemed to gleam as if lit from within.

Landers stared at it in disbelief, his eyes bulging. His hands twitched over the money and then clenched into fists before slowly withdrawing.

"Damn you, Quentin."

"You've already said that once. You really shouldn't repeat yourself so often. It makes for a boring conversation." Quentin's long fingers neatly stacked the money. He seemed oblivious to the hungry way Landers's eyes followed the bills as he tucked them inside his coat.

"Here." The stranger handed a bill to Colin, giving him a friendly smile. "My apologies for keeping you up well past the time when civilized men are abed."

"Thank you," Colin murmured, taking the bill. It wasn't until the man had turned away that he looked at it and realized that he was holding one hundred dollars, more than two months' wages. He started to call the stranger back, but stopped. Considering the thousands the man had just pocketed as casually as if they were pennies, the tip was probably not a mistake.

With the stranger's departure, the small crowd dispersed. Landers had left the table abruptly, striding off with quick, angry steps. Colin found himself hoping the stranger had the sense to pick up a hack. He wouldn't want to be on the street at this hour after having just won so heavily from Joseph Landers. Landers struck him as likely to have any number of undesirable acquaintances who'd not object to knocking a man over the head.

Minutes later Colin shrugged into his coat and left the saloon. There'd be little more money to be earned tonight. What small spark had enlivened the night had left with the stranger.

Outside, the air was cold and damp and he hunched his shoulders, buttoning his too-thin coat against the chill. He lingered near the wall of the saloon, waiting until a horse and buggy had passed by, the driver huddled beneath the warmth of a thick coat and blanket.

Fog swirled around his legs as he stepped into the street. The light from the street lamps struggled futilely against the white mist, winning only a tiny patch of ground before giving up the battle. Long stretches of dingy gray marked the distance between the lamps. Objects were only half seen until you stepped right up to them.

The fog slowed Colin's stride only slightly. He'd traveled this road so many times, he could have walked it blindfolded. He'd grown accustomed to the thick, white fog that often blanketed the city, cloaking everything in pale tendrils of dampness. There was a certain pleasure to these late-night hours. With the fog shrouding everything in mystery, he might have been the only person in the city.

He was just a few short blocks from the saloon when a vague sound caught his attention—a muffled shout. He slowed his stride, cocking his head trying to pinpoint the sound. The fog distorted sound as well as sight.

He hesitated at the mouth of an alleyway. Through the haze, he could just discern the vague outlines of four men. If there was one thing Colin had learned in this life, it was that it paid to mind your own business, and that was a rule that applied even more here on the Barbary Coast. People who forgot it were lucky if they lived to regret their nosiness.

Still, it looked as if the odds here were far from

even. Three men faced a fourth and Colin doubted that they were having a cozy chat. He hesitated a moment longer, knowing that the wise choice was to walk away. Katie would be lying awake, waiting for him, though she thought that was her secret. He had a responsibility to her.

The three closed in on the one and the sound of fists striking flesh echoed eerily down the alley. Muttering a curse at his own stupidity, Colin turned and ran toward the men.

The fight was short and savage. The ruffians hadn't been prepared for two opponents and Colin's entrance into the battle threw them off balance. He bruised his fist against an unshaven jaw before burying the other fist in a belly grown soft with too much gin. There was a muffled grunt from his opponent, and then a cry of pain from where the other two still faced their intended victim.

Colin dodged a blow that would have laid him out and planted another solid fist on the man's chin. Glancing around as the ruffian staggered back, he saw that the victim had dispatched one of his opponents and was now facing the second.

With the odds suddenly evened up, the thugs lost their taste for the game. The two still standing turned and ran, leaving their compatriot stretched out on the hard ground.

The silence was suddenly as thick as the fog. At first, all Colin could hear was the ragged beating of his own heart. His hands ached and he hoped they wouldn't stiffen up to the point where he couldn't handle a deck of cards.

"I thank you, sir. Your aid was most well-timed."

Colin turned toward the husky voice, aware of a niggling sense of familiarity. But in the density of the haze he could not identify the face.

"It seems they had little stomach for a fight when the odds were not so heavily in their favor," Colin said.

"Well, it's my good fortune that they weren't more dedicated to their task." He broke off, reaching one hand up to his shoulder and swaying slightly.

"You're hurt," Colin exclaimed, stepping over the form of the fallen man with no more than a cursory glance. It was enough to tell him that the ruffian lived, which was probably more than he deserved.

"A matter of a small knife wound. Nothing too serious, I think."

"You should have it tended to." Colin glanced around the alley and came to a decision. He'd already interfered more than sanity recommended. Now the man was hurt and there was certainly no way to tell just how badly until they got him to a source of light. "Come with me. My sister will tend to you."

"It's not so bad that it can't wait for attention. I doubt your sister will be overjoyed to have you arrive on her doorstep with a stranger in tow and ask her to tend his wounds."

Despite the light amusement in his tone, Colin saw him sway again. He bent to pick up the man's hat, dusting it on his leg before handing it to the stranger.

"Katie won't mind. She'd not forgive me for leaving you here, alone and bleeding, at the mercy of those men should they return."

"Well, I certainly would not want to be a cause of bringing your sister's wrath down on your head. That would be churlish of me after you came to my aid in such a splendid manner.''

He took the hat Colin proffered and set it on his head before bending to pick up the walking stick that had been wrenched away in the fighting. A quick intake of breath said that the movement had been unwise and he didn't spurn the hand that Colin set under his arm to steady him as he straightened.

They'd gone only a short distance when Colin became aware that the stranger's unsteadiness was caused as much by alcohol as by any damage done in the fight. He frowned, wondering if this was such a good idea after all. His doubts grew even stronger when they stepped beneath a lantern and he caught a glimpse of the stranger's face. It was the man from the Rearing Stallion, the fair-haired gambler who'd walked away with his pockets full.

Something told him that he was going to regret bringing this man home. He had a feeling this stranger was not the sort of gentleman he should be introducing to his sister, particularly not at nearly four in the morning. Still, it was too late to change his mind now and there was no denying that the man was hurt.

KATIE STARTED UP in bed at the sound of footsteps in the hallway. She'd dozed off still listening for Colin's return and now her heart was pounding with the suddenness of her awakening.

The footsteps stopped outside the door and she reached up one hand to clutch the neck of her nightdress. Colin would be alone, yet she could hear the mutter of voices. Thieves? But surely thieves would not be so loud, nor would they waste their time on a building such as this, where they could hardly expect to find anything worth their while.

"Katie?" Her brother's soft voice followed on the sound of a key in the lock and then the creak of the door. "Katie, I've brought a man who's hurt. Will you help?"

Katie swung her legs off the narrow bed, reaching for the light flannel wrapper she'd laid ready for morning. Buttoning the collar high on her throat, she patted a hand over her hair in a vague attempt to curb its thick waywardness.

She brushed aside the curtain that separated her bed from the rest of the room, blinking in the sudden light as Colin lit the lamp. Colin turned from the table, an explanation on his tongue, but Katie hardly heard him. She was staring at the stranger who stood near the door.

He was tall, taller even than Colin. His shoulders were broad, filling out the formal black jacket in a way that must have made his tailor happy. His hair was a shade that seemed not quite gold and not quite brown but was somewhere between the two. His features were strong, too strong to be considered handsome perhaps, but compelling all the same.

But it was his eyes that threatened to steal her breath away. They were blue, but more than blue. They were deep in color, not like a summer sky but more like a sapphire she'd seen once.

Katie flushed as those eyes swept over her thinly clad figure. The look was appreciative without being lascivious, and when his eyes met hers, there was a spark in them that told her he liked what he'd seen.

Katie was ashamed to find that her heart beat a little faster at the thought.

"I'm sorry to intrude on you in this boorish manner, ma'am. I'm afraid your brother overestimates the extent of my injury." He swept a battered silk hat from his head and bent low in a bow. The elegance of the gesture was marred by the fact that he had to clutch at the edge of the table to keep from losing his balance. Colin, just turning away from adjusting the wick on the lamp, caught at his arm, lending him support.

Katie's eyes found the dark stain on the sleeve of his jacket and she hurried forward.

"Help the gentleman to a seat, Colin, and let me take a look at that arm."

Colin eased the stranger to a chair, then stepped back and watched as Katie knelt in front of him. His doubts about bringing the man here were even stronger now that it was too late. He didn't like the way the man looked at his sister and he didn't like the way Katie had looked at him in that first moment.

The man was a gambler and a drinker—and who knew what else? And setting all that aside, there was no doubting that he came from a class far above their reach. Everything about the man spoke of money, something the McBrides had never had much of. They could have nothing in common with a man who wore such fine clothes and gambled with such a fine lack of regard for winning or losing. And it wouldn't do for Katie to be setting her sights so high.

Colin ran his hand through his dark hair, feeling weariness sweep over him. It wasn't only the lateness of the hour, it was the burden of responsibility he felt.

He was all that Katie had now. It was up to him to see that she had a good life ahead of her.

"Colin, get me some water in a bowl and bring my sewing basket." As she tugged experimentally at the blood-soaked sleeve, she told her patient, "I'm afraid removing your coat is going to be more than a bit painful, sir."

"Cut it away."

"Oh, no, I don't think that will be necessary. I'm sure it can be saved. A bit of mending and it will be good as new."

"It's not worth worrying about," he said casually. "Just cut the sleeve loose. I'm in no mood to try and pull it off."

"But that will ruin it and it's such a fine fabric."

"I have others and I'm afraid the fabric of my skin is a bit more important to me at the moment. A sharp knife will solve the problem in an instant."

Colin set down the sewing basket and a basin of water next to Katie, stepping back without a word. Reluctantly, Katie picked up her scissors, still hesitant about ruining a garment as fine as the one the stranger wore.

"I assure you it's not going to leave me without clothing," he said quietly.

She met his eyes, finding a certain understanding there, as if he knew that clothing was a precious commodity in her world. Her pale skin flushed pink at the thought that this man saw her poverty and perhaps pitied her for it.

With a quick movement, she split the sleeve up the side, exposing the white silk of his shirt. She didn't even mention that the shirt too could be repaired but disposed of it as efficiently as she had the jacket. Her movements gentled as she eased the fabric away from the deep slash in the upper arm.

Studying the wound, Katie tried not to notice the muscles that rippled under the golden skin she'd bared, more muscles than seemed right for a man who wore silk hats and expensively tailored evening clothes.

"It should have a stitch or two to make sure that it heals properly. If you'll trust me to do the job, I'll see to it."

She was sponging the blood from around the wound as she spoke, her light touch contrasting with the determined briskness of her words. When the stranger didn't say anything, she reluctantly shifted her eyes to his face. He was looking at her hair, which spilled in fiery disarray across her shoulders.

"Your hair is the most beautiful color I've ever seen, though I'm sure you think it forward of me to mention it."

Katie's cheeks flushed. "I do think it forward of you," she said bluntly. "Will you be wanting me to tend to your arm or not?"

He shifted his gaze from her hair to her face, not sparing even a glance for the gash in his arm. "Yes, please."

He said if softly, sweetly, like a child requesting a treat before supper. Hastily, Katie bent her head over her sewing box, not looking up again until she had a threaded needle in hand.

"You must hold still while I set the stitches. 'Tis likely to hurt a bit," she warned him as she motioned to Colin to shift the light closer. Lifting the chimney off, she held the needle over the flame.

"I shall be steady as a rock. If I may be completely honest, I do believe I have imbibed enough liquor this past night to prevent any but the greatest of pains from bothering me. Please, do not concern yourself."

Though Katie didn't doubt that he'd had enough liquor to numb his senses, she nibbled on her lower lip as she drew the edges of the wound together and set the first stitch. It wasn't the first time she'd applied her skills with a needle to the mending of a human being. Small injuries were common enough in the theater but money was not. So theater people were inclined to do for themselves rather than call a doctor.

True to his word, the stranger didn't flinch, though he sucked in his breath sharply a time or two. Katie didn't dare look at his face as she carefully stitched the wound closed.

No one said a word until she'd set the last stitch and clipped the thread. She sat back on her heels, studying the work a moment before nodding her head.

"With a little care, you should do. 'Twould be best if you tried not to do any heavy lifting with that arm for a week or two, just long enough to give the flesh time to knit solid."

The man turned his head to look at his arm, the neat row of stitches slashing across the tanned skin.

"You've done a fine job. And I thank you for it."

"It would be better thanks if you'd stay out of dark alleys where trouble is likely to seek a man out."

"You're quite right. If it hadn't been for your brother, I've no doubt that I'd have been beyond the need for patching. I thank you both." He frowned suddenly, watching as Katie put away her needle and scissors. "I don't even know who I'm thanking."

Katie rose, shaking out the skirts of her wrapper and stepping back as the stranger stood up. Odd, how he seemed to dominate the room.

"I'm Colin McBride and this is my sister, Katie." Colin made the introduction reluctantly. He didn't lay claim to the second sight his father had always sworn to have but he had a strong feeling that bringing this stranger here had been a mistake.

"Quentin Sterling at your service." The stranger bowed low. Katie dipped a small curtsy, feeling a bit ridiculous in her wrapper and nightgown, her hair all willy-nilly on her shoulders.

"It's a pleasure to make your acquaintance," she said politely.

"I think your good manners outweigh your honesty, ma'am." The twinkle in his eyes took any insult from the words. "This is hardly the way I'd choose to meet such a charming and beautiful young lady."

Colin stiffened beside her. "I'll walk out with you. I'm sure we'll be able to find a hack."

Quentin's eyes met his, understanding in their depths. "You're quite right. I've taken up much more of your time than I've any right to."

He reached to pick up his hat, bowing again to Katie. "I thank you, ma'am, for your kindness and your skill with a needle."

Colin opened the door, leaving no time for Katie's response, if she'd had one. Quentin Sterling's eyes met hers for one long moment before he turned away, stepping through the door her brother held open.

Katie stood staring at the blank panel, one hand pressed to her bosom, feeling slightly breathless. After a moment, she shook her head and turned back to the cubbyhole that sheltered her bed. She had a feeling Colin was going to want to discuss their visitor with her, but she didn't want to talk about him.

She wasn't a foolish young girl. She knew as well as Colin did that she'd never see Mr. Quentin Sterling again, but would it hurt so very much to dream a little of what it might be like to have a man like that fall in love with her?

Chapter Two

When the church bell struck five, Katie dragged her eyes open, focusing sleepily on the cracked and peeling ceiling. If she closed her eyes again, she could sleep a few more minutes and perhaps she could take the trolley to work this morning. Surely it wouldn't be such a terrible extravagance just this once.

With a groan, she forced herself upright. If she took a trolley this morning, she'd surely want to do the same tomorrow and the day after that. Bad habits were easily begun but harder to stop. And the pennies were better saved for the future.

She swung her legs off the bed and stretched her arms over her head to work the kinks out of her back. Ignoring the temptation to fall back onto the thin mattress for just one more minute of sleep, Katie stood up, reaching for her wrapper. If she hurried, she might be able to use the bathroom down the hall before the other tenants stirred. Slipping her feet into a pair of satin slippers—mementoes of a successful run at a fine Boston theater—she eased through the curtain that surrounded her bed, tiptoeing through the living area.

Colin slept on a pallet made of a thick folded quilt.

A blanket was drawn up over his shoulders, blocking out the morning chill. Katie lifted the towel she'd laid ready the night before and slipped out the door.

There was no one in the bathroom, a rare occurrence with nearly fifteen families sharing the meager facilities. Mindful that it wouldn't be long before there were others queuing up in the hall, she hurried through her ablutions.

Drying her face on the rough towel, Katie suddenly remembered the one time they'd stayed at the Waldorf-Astoria. That had been during her brief, never-to-be-forgotten employment on the hallowed boards of Broadway. Her parents had celebrated with the same enthusiastic joy with which they embraced every other aspect of life. They'd taken a room at the elegant hotel, putting on airs that the Vanderbilts themselves would have envied. The towels there had been of the finest, softest linen, gently soothing the moisture from the skin instead of removing it by brute force.

Katie shook her head, dismissing the old memories. That had been another time and place. She folded the towel neatly and tightened the tie of her wrapper before stepping out into the hallway. There was a small queue of people waiting their turn at the facilities and she nodded pleasantly to one or two.

She eased back into the apartment as quietly as possible though Colin would, like as not, sleep through a cavalry charge. He'd turned in his sleep and now faced the room. Katie hesitated a moment, noting the lines drawn too deeply about his mouth. He looked older than his twenty-five years. Not even sleep could erase the worry from his face.

She was frowning as she slipped behind the curtain

that surrounded her bed. She'd have given anything right then to have inherited a bit more of her parents' optimism, their belief that something better always waited around the next curve in the road.

She stepped into a plain gray dress and drew it up over her shoulders, settling it in place before slipping the buttons through the buttonholes. She'd have much preferred to be wearing one of the new shirtwaists that were gaining such popularity. To have a skirt separate from the bodice seemed a wonderful thing but Mrs. Ferriweather thought them an abomination—much too mannish and certainly not something one of "her girls" would ever wear.

She dragged a brush through her hair with ruthless force before gathering the thick mass into a knot. Holding it against the back of her head, she caught a glimpse of herself in the cracked mirror that hung beside the bed. *Your hair is the most beautiful color I've ever seen.*

The voice in her head was deep, with a whiskey rasp to it. She'd been trying very hard not to think of the injured stranger, not to remember the blue of his eyes or the broad shoulders that had filled his dinner jacket to such perfection. Quentin Sterling. The name bespoke quality, even if his manner and the cut of his clothes hadn't already done so.

Shaking her head, she pushed pins into her hair to secure the thick knot at the back of her head. She was a fool to be letting a man like that into her dreams. No one knew better than she that nothing could come of it.

Pushing Mr. Quentin Sterling out of her thoughts, she checked her reflection one last time, making sure that she looked neat as a pin. Even if she was only to be bent over her sewing all day, Mrs. Ferriweather expected all her girls to be tidy.

Slipping through the outer room on tiptoes, she let herself out and hurried down the hallway. Though the church bells were proclaiming only half past the hour, she'd have a brisk walk to get to the shop on time.

Tattered threads of fog drifted through the streets. Glancing at the gray sky, Katie tugged her wrap closer about her shoulders. It didn't look as if there'd be much sun today. Not that it would matter much to her, since she wasn't likely to get out again until near dark.

Climbing up one of the city's famous hills, Katie tried not to pant in an unladylike fashion. Why couldn't Colin have settled someplace flat? Reaching the top, she paused to catch her breath. She looked back down the hill she'd just climbed. The city spread out, seemingly at her feet. In the distance, she could see the bay. The sun had burned the last of the fog, leaving the waters blue and sparkling.

But not as blue as Quentin Sterling's eyes.

The thought slipped in, unwelcome. Exasperated, she turned away from the magnificence of the view and stepped out briskly. Almost too briskly. As she stepped off the curb to cross the street, a raucous blast of a horn sent her jumping back, nearly losing her balance as she sought the safety of the walkway. The automobile flew by her at a dizzying speed, the driver shrouded in coat, hat and goggles so that it was a wonder he could move at all beneath all those layers.

He didn't bother to glance her way as he sped off down the street, the gleaming ivory of his vehicle catching the sun. Katie watched him out of sight, one hand pressed to her bosom as she tried to still the pounding of her heart.

She'd not liked the new mode of travel even before her parents' death. She liked it even less now. Automobiles were nasty, smelly vehicles, little more than playthings for the rich and not likely to be anything more.

Looking both ways, she hurried across the street. It must be nearly seven o'clock, and Mrs. Ferriweather believed in punctuality the way others believed in the power of prayer.

Katie had never been late. In fact, she made it a point to be the first one to arrive more often than not. And she knew that her efforts had not gone unnoticed, which was exactly what she wanted. Mrs. Ferriweather's assistant was to be wed in the summer. Naturally, she'd be leaving her position then and Katie had hopes that Mrs. Ferriweather might consider her as a replacement for Miss Lewis. Her age would be a strike against her, even though Mrs. Ferriweather thought she was twenty-two.

Still, she'd done her best to prove herself indispensable over the past few months. As an assistant instead of one of the seamstresses, she'd make more money and get the experience she would need if she was ever to open a shop of her own.

When she'd come to San Francisco, she hadn't known anything beyond the fact that her future wasn't on the stage. She'd taken a long, hard look at her skills and put to use the only talent she had besides song and dance.

Mrs. Ferriweather's establishment was much too elegant to be called a dress shop. She catered to only the very finest clientele, turning lengths of silk and soft woolens into sophisticated gowns in the latest fashions. At first, she'd refused to hire Katie, saying she didn't need another seamstress, but Katie had persisted, using every acting skill she'd acquired to make it seem as if Mrs. Ferriweather needed her more than she needed Mrs. Ferriweather. That had gotten her foot in the door and her talent with a needle had gotten her the job.

So, for the past six months, she'd spent ten hours a day, six days a week plying her needle. The pay was better than she might have made elsewhere—nearly thirty-five dollars per month. And if she could take over Miss Lewis's position in the summer... Well, maybe she and Colin could afford to rent a little house somewhere. A real home.

By noon, Katie's back ached. On one side of the room, several sewing machines hummed as the girls worked the treadles back and forth. Sometimes Katie worked at one of the machines but her talent for fine embroidery meant that she spent most of her time working by hand.

Today, she was applying an elaborate design of soutache braid to a pale green jacket. The design had been traced onto the garment but it required hours of careful stitching to tack the braid into place.

"Ladies, I have some wonderful news." Katie looked up as Mrs. Ferriweather stepped into the room, her ample frame fairly quivering with excitement. She waited until all eyes were on her, the hum of the sewing machines halted and every needle stilled.

"We have been asked to provide a seamstress to assist in preparation for one of the season's biggest weddings. Miss Ann Sterling is to wed Mr. Jonathon Drake in less than three weeks. It seems that the seamstress the Sterlings had hired has fallen and broken her wrist. Such a pity,'' she added dutifully.

Katie heard little beyond the name. Sterling. Was it possible that they were any relation to *her* Quentin Sterling? Not that he was really hers, of course, but she couldn't help but feel a bit possessive. There were probably several Sterling families in San Francisco, and there was no reason to think that he was a member of this particular one.

"Since we have provided several gowns to Mrs. Sterling and she has been gracious enough to express her satisfaction with our work, she has requested that we provide her with a replacement for Miss Smith. Naturally, it is of utmost importance that our work be of the very highest quality. I'm sure I don't need to tell you that providing even a part of the trousseau for Miss Sterling would be quite a feather in our cap.''

She paused, beaming at her workers fondly. Katie hardly dared to breathe. She wanted to be the one chosen to work for the Sterlings. She wanted it more than she'd wanted anything in a long time. It was crazy. It probably wasn't even the same family. Even if it was, it could make no possible difference to her. A man like Quentin Sterling would never look at a girl like Katie McBride.

But knowing it was foolish didn't stop her from wanting it. And when Mrs. Ferriweather's eyes fell on her, Katie was sure her desire must be plain to see.

"It will certainly be a great deal of work, ladies. And long hours. Though much of the work will be done here in the shop, Mrs. Sterling wishes to have a seamstress in residence at her home. She's offered to provide a room where you'll be able to stay if you don't wish to travel home each night.''

Was it Katie's imagination or was Mrs. Ferriweather's eye lingering on her? She looked down, smoothing the crease from the fine wool, laying a section of braid in place absently. It was bad luck to want something so much.

''Miss McBride?'' Katie jumped at the sound of her name. She'd lost track of her employer's words.

''Yes, ma'am?'' She looked up, hoping her expression was calm.

''I believe you live with your brother, don't you?''

''Yes, ma'am, I do.''

''Would he object to you taking such a position temporarily? It would mean a few additional dollars, of course, to compensate for the extra hours you would be required to spend. Do you think he would allow you to take such an assignment?''

''Yes, ma'am.'' Despite the breathless feeling that threatened to overcome her, Katie's voice was steady.

Only someone who knew her very well indeed could have guessed at the foolish pounding of her heart. It couldn't possibly be the same family. But if it was?

''MAYBE I SHOULDN'T have come home.''

Tobias MacNamara looked up from the chess board, focusing faded but still shrewd eyes on his grandson. Quentin was staring out the window at another foggy winter day. It had been almost a week since San Francisco had gotten more than a glimpse of the sun and Quentin had been getting more restless with every day that passéd. But Tobias didn't think it was the gloomy weather that had his grandson as jumpy as a cat on coals.

"Why *did* you come home, boy?"

Quentin stirred restlessly, pretending not to notice when his grandfather moved an ivory knight in a manner that was unconventional, to say the least. One of the old man's chief pleasures was in seeing if he could sneak a few "unusual" moves past his opponent.

Why *had* he come home?

"I don't know." He moved a bishop, glowering at the ivory and ebony pieces as if his restlessness were their fault.

"Must've had a reason, boy. You didn't come home for this shindig of your mother's." Tobias's contempt for the wedding preparations was clear. "If you had any sense, you'd have stayed away until Ann tied the knot and she and that weak-chinned nincompoop she's caught have sailed off on their honeymoon."

Quentin smiled at the old man's disgust. "Jonathan is hardly a nincompoop, Grandfather. Ann tells me that he holds a responsible position in his father's shipping firm."

"Hah! Jonathan Drake was born a nincompoop and he'll die a nincompoop. I knew his grandfather—had a claim near mine in 'forty-nine. Good man, a little too soft, but a good man. He started that business, made a good beginning and then got drunk one night, tripped getting out of his carriage and broke his fool neck. The son inherited and he's done fair enough with the business. Shipped around the Horn with them a time or two myself.

"Went with a shipment of cowhides myself back in

'fifty-eight or so. Now that was a voyage.'' The old man's eyes grew distant with memories. "Caught us a storm just off the Horn. Captain thought we were done for but we made it out without losing a hand and I made a tidy profit on those hides. Now I hear they're talking about building some kind of Canal across Panama. That Frenchman tried and couldn't do it but maybe Roosevelt can figure out a way.''

"I don't think the president is actually planning on designing the thing himself, Grandfather.''

"Of course not. But none of this has anything to do with why you came home.'' Tobias waved his hand impatiently, returning to the original subject.

"I thought the least I could do was return for my sister's wedding,'' Quentin said. "Besides, winter in Wyoming can be a bit harrowing. I decided I could use a break.''

"A break, is it? Or did you want a taste of your old life again? That sniveling wimp of a cousin of yours couldn't wait to tell your mother all about your return to your wicked ways.''

Quentin's smile held an unpleasant edge. "It was quite a surprise to find Joseph across the table from me.''

"He seemed to think it an unpleasant one.''

"A man who plays as badly as he does shouldn't play at all.''

"Do you still blame him for young Alice's death?'' Tobias asked gruffly.

Quentin's fingers tightened over the captured rook he'd been toying with. The look he shot the old man would have been enough to set a lesser man back on his heels.

"I do not wish to discuss Alice."

"No, I know you don't. You haven't discussed her in eight years, not since she died. Well, time is supposed to heal all wounds and I think it's time you took a look at that one. You may find it's healed more than you think.

"And though I think Joseph Landers is a liar and a cheat and probably not above murder, the girl's death wasn't his doing."

"Why are you bringing this up? And why are you defending Landers? As I recall, you've threatened more than once to forbid him to ever set foot in this house again."

"That I have. And if it hadn't been for your mother's weeping and carrying on, I'd have stuck by that. How a daughter of mine could be so fond of such an irritating little twerp..." He broke off shaking his head over the vagaries of females. "But that should be enough to convince you Alice's death wasn't his fault. You know how your mother felt about Alice, how she felt about your engagement. The fact is, boy, there was nothing anyone could have done but what Landers did."

"He left her there alone," Quentin said, his jaw tight.

"He went for help," Tobias corrected. "When she fell through the ice, he couldn't pull her up himself. That damned gown must have weighed fifty pounds and the ice was rotten. *You* couldn't have done anything but what he did."

Quentin stood up, the memories roiling inside him. He couldn't argue with his grandfather's words, but neither could he bring himself to agree with them. For so many years he'd focused his anger on Joseph Landers and heaven knew the man deserved it on a hundred other counts. He'd simply never let himself accept that, in this one instance, he might be innocent of wrongdoing.

Because, if Joseph wasn't to blame, he might have to accept some of the responsibility for Alice's death himself. If he hadn't gone away... If they'd married as everyone had expected...

Quentin stared out at the wispy fog that draped Nob Hill in a gossamer blanket, but his eyes were on the past. He'd been in the Yukon, on the tail end of the great gold rush when word of his fiancée's death had reached him. By the time he received the letter, she'd been dead and buried nearly a month.

She'd gone to New York with his family for the New Year celebrations, gone to see in the last year of the old century. She'd been ice-skating with several of her friends, including his sister Ann, hardly more than a child then. When she'd skated too near the center of the lake, the ice—not yet solid enough to bear her weight—had given way.

Joseph had gone for help, but by the time they were able to pull Alice from the water, she was half-frozen. The chill turned into pneumonia and she'd died within a week. There'd been nothing anyone could do, everyone had agreed on that. It was a terrible tragedy.

Quentin had known Alice Mason since they were children. And he'd known they were going to marry since he was fifteen and she was twelve. They might have been wed already but for the restlessness that stirred in him, an urge to see more of the world. And

Alice had understood that restlessness. She'd be waiting, she told him.

So he'd gone to Alaska. Less than a year before, word had come of a great gold strike on the Klondike. The reports were that nearly two tons of gold had been unloaded on the Seattle docks. Some said it was the richest gold strike in the world, with nuggets just lying on the ground waiting to be picked up by any enterprising young man.

Quentin was not so foolish as to believe that, but it seemed as good a place as any to start seeing the world. And see it he had. He'd seen men gone mad with gold fever, unable to believe that their fortune wasn't just lying about. He'd found a little gold himself, barely enough to pay his expenses, and he'd counted himself lucky to find that much.

But the price he'd paid had been far too high. He'd come home only long enough to visit Alice's grave, needing to see it before he could make himself believe in the reality of her death. And then he'd left again. There was a war beginning with Spain and he'd joined a bunch of cowboys, college students and misfits, who'd come to be called the Rough Riders.

And when Cuba was safely free of Spain's domination, he'd left the service and traveled around the world, just as he'd planned before Alice's death. He'd gambled in every back alley in every port he'd visited. He'd worked his passage more often than purchased it and he'd spent what money he made. He'd been home a time or two to listen to his father tell him he was going to hell in a handbasket, to have his mother look at him with tears in her eyes and his grandfather with understanding.

He turned from the window abruptly. "Maybe Alice's death wasn't Joseph's fault, but it's no doubt the first time he's been blamed for something he *wasn't* guilty of."

"I'll not argue with that." Tobias leaned back in his chair, reaching for one of the cigars the doctor had forbidden him to smoke. When a man got to his age, there were few enough pleasures in life. He wasn't going to give up one of those left him.

He lit the cigar, puffing at the rich Cuban tobacco for a moment as he watched his grandson move restlessly around the room. Something was on the boy's mind, there was no doubt of that. Of all his family, Quentin was the only one worth a damn. His daughter was an empty-headed fool, who'd married a stodgy businessman with the imagination of a turnip. His granddaughter hadn't a thought in her head but fashion, and now her wedding.

But Quentin—Quentin was the son he'd never had, a true kindred spirit. Let the rest of them wring their hands and weep and wail over the boy wasting his life. He'd understood Quentin's anger, his pain and his need to work it out in his own way. Everything had turned out well enough.

Four years ago, he'd won title to a ranch in Wyoming, drawing to fill an inside straight at poker. Tobias smiled at the memory, remembering a time when he'd drawn to fill his own inside straights, though cards had never been his weakness. But there was more than one way to gamble and he'd done his share.

Maybe Quentin had always wanted a ranch, or maybe he was just tired of roaming the world, belonging nowhere. Whatever the reason, he hadn't gambled the ranch away sight unseen, nor had he sold it. He'd gone to take a look at it and there he'd stayed.

Until now.

"You still haven't told me why you came home."

Quentin looked up from the fist-sized piece of gold ore he'd been studying. The first chunk of ore his grandfather had ever mined, taken from the Sutter's Mill strike back in 'forty-nine, the strike that had founded the family fortune. How many times had he heard that story, sitting on a hassock at his grandfather's knee, listening wide-eyed to tales of days gone by?

He set the ore down, slipping his hand into the pocket of his neat gray trousers. If anyone would understand his purpose in coming back here, it was Tobias.

"I've decided to marry."

Tobias said nothing for a moment, puffing on his cigar, studying Quentin through the veil of smoke. "Well, you're of an age for it. A man should have a wife and children. It steadies him, gives him a purpose in life. Who's the girl?"

"I don't know yet. I've come home to find a wife."

"Have you mentioned this to your mother?"

"No. I thought I'd wait until after Ann's wedding. Once that's done, I thought maybe she'd like to throw a few parties or something, introduce me to some eligible females. I've met few enough of those in my wanderings," he said with a half smile.

Tobias studied the glowing end of his cigar for a moment before fixing his gaze on Quentin. "Don't do it, boy. Don't say a word to your mother about this. Oh, don't get me wrong, I'm sure she'd be delighted to have a party or two. In fact, she'd probably throw a ball if you wanted. But you're not going to find a wife in this house.''

Startled, Quentin crossed the room to lean his arms on the back of the richly upholstered wing chair. The chessboard lay forgotten between them.

''Why not? You're not going to try and tell me that Mother doesn't know any eligible females?''

''She knows plenty of eligible females, but it all depends on what you want them to be eligible for. The girls she'd introduce you to would know all about going to parties and running a big house with plenty of servants. They'll know just how many spoons to put beside each plate and what sort of crystal is the most fashionable in any given year. Are you planning on that sort of life?''

''No, I'm going back to the ranch as soon as I've found a wife. I need a girl who can run a home five miles from the nearest neighbor.''

''Well, you're not going to find a girl like that at any party your mother gives,'' Tobias told him bluntly.

Quentin sat down, hearing the truth of his grandfather's words. It had all seemed so simple back in Wyoming. He'd get his mother to introduce him around. He'd find a girl he could imagine spending his life with—not a love match, God knows. He'd had that once and it was simply too painful to risk again. No, he wasn't looking to fall in love. He was looking for more of a partnership, someone to build a life with. They'd get married and he'd take her back to Wyoming, though he wasn't opposed to a short honeymoon if it was important to her.

It had never occurred to him that none of the daughters of his mother's friends were likely to be the sort of girl who'd know how to make a home in the primitive surroundings he could offer. Nor would they want to try. He stared at his grandfather in silence, seeing all his plans crumbling.

A soft tapping on the door interrupted his thoughts. Tobias glanced at the clock and his thick white brows hooked together.

"Nearly four o'clock and I always have my tea at three," he muttered. "I swear this household is falling to pieces. Come in," he barked.

Quentin paid little attention as the door was pushed open and a maid entered bearing a heavy tray.

"Your tea, sir."

"And only an hour late," Tobias said sharply. "Where have you been, girl, dallying in the butler's pantry with one of the stable boys?"

The tea hit the table with a little more force than was strictly necessary. "I'm sorry if your tea is late."

"Oh, don't worry. I'm aware that I'm the least important member of this household. I suppose I should consider myself lucky that anyone remembered me at all," he said with heavy sarcasm.

"I'm sure no one considers you unimportant, sir."

"What happened to the girl who usually brings me my tea? She sick? Or did that dragon of a housekeeper fire her for sneezing out of turn?"

"Edith is polishing the silver, I believe."

Something about the sound of her voice tugged at Quentin's memory. Hadn't he heard that particular voice before? It was a little deeper than average with a soft husky note—a bedroom voice. And he was sure he'd heard it somewhere else.

Tobias was still mumbling about the lack of attention to an old man's needs. The girl stood before him, waiting politely for him to finish before going on about her duties.

He could see little beyond a neat back wearing one of the dull gray gowns all the maids wore. Her hair was gathered in a heavy knot at the back of her head, though a few strands of dark auburn had slipped from beneath the plain cap she wore. The color was familiar. He'd seen it before but it hadn't been bundled in a knot. It had been lying about her shoulders and he'd wanted to touch it, to see if it was as warm and soft as it looked.

"You're new here, aren't you?" Tobias asked.

"Yes, sir. I'm the new seamstress, brought in to help with the wedding."

"And a very fine seamstress, I'd say," Quentin said, suddenly placing the voice. He reached up to touch his shoulder.

Katie jumped as if the sound of his voice was a whip cracked over her head. Hidden by the arms of the wing chair as he was, she hadn't even realized that there was anyone but the old man in the room.

She turned, feeling the color leave her face when she saw who had spoken her name. Quentin stood up, a smile lighting his eyes. He was just as handsome as she remembered. The ruined evening coat and silk shirt were gone, as were the dust and bloodstains that had given him such a dangerous air.

Now he wore a dark jacket and snowy white shirt, his trousers were neatly creased and the shine on his shoes was dazzling. His thick, golden-brown hair was neatly combed into place.

"I didn't think I'd see you again. What a coincidence."

"Yes, sir." She got the words out with difficulty, as the color rushed back into her face until she was sure she must be as red as the carpet beneath her feet.

"I was going to come back and thank you properly, you know," Quentin said. "But I couldn't find you once I'd sobered up." His smile was self-deprecating. "That will teach me to drink more than I should. I'd thought of going back to the Rearing Stallion to see if I might see your brother again and thank him for his part in the evening's events, but I got the distinct impression he didn't approve of me."

"I'm sure that's not true," Katie mumbled, hiding her shaking hands at her sides, focusing her eyes on his neatly draped cravat. In the two weeks since she'd joined the Sterling household, she'd heard enough mention of Mr. Quentin to know that he was here, but as the days passed and their paths hadn't crossed, she'd begun to forget the reason she'd been so anxious to come here. Now, here he was and she was as tongue-tied as a child.

"I must go," she muttered. Bobbing in a stiff curtsy, she fled, pretending she didn't hear him say her name.

"What was that about?" Tobias demanded of his grandson. Quentin was staring at the door with a strange expression in his eyes.

"Excuse me, Grandfather. I'll be right back." His departure was abrupt. Tobias stared after him, frowning.

Katie was halfway down the hall when she heard
him behind her.

"Wait." The quiet call had the opposite effect from
what he intended. She picked up her already brisk pace
until she was nearly running. She wasn't ready to see
him. She'd been a fool to come here in the first place.

"Miss McBride. Katie." This time the command
was louder, impossible to ignore. She slowed, her eyes
turning longingly to the narrow flight of stairs that led
to the upper floor and the sanctuary of the sewing
room. If only she could have reached that. Surely he'd
not have followed her. But she could hardly go on
pretending to be deaf, especially when he showed no
sign of giving up the pursuit.

She turned reluctantly. Seeing that she'd stopped,
Quentin slowed his quick steps to something more
suited to the elegance of his mother's hallway. Katie
waited until he'd stopped in front of her and then curtsied.

"What can I do for you, Mr. Sterling?" She fixed
her gaze on the top button of his coat, refusing to lift
her eyes any higher.

"I thought you might be curious to know how your
patient progressed," he said lightly.

"How is your arm?" Despite herself, Katie's tone
softened.

"Almost healed, thank you. It was quite sore for a
few days. But I suppose you think that's no more than
I deserve."

"I certainly don't think any man deserves to be attacked by a bunch of common thieves," she said angrily, her eyes darting to his face.

"That's nice to know. You were so disapproving of

me that I rather thought you resented your brother's bringing me to you.''

"I'd not have turned a wounded dog away from the door." It wasn't until she saw Quentin wince at the comparison that she realized how her words had sounded. "Heavens! I didn't mean to say that you were not better than a dog. You certainly are. After all, you're a Sterling and that alone would... Not that you yourself aren't..." She trailed off miserably when Quentin lifted his hand.

"Please. Don't go on. I believe I understand what you're trying to say. You'd have done the same for anyone, which does credit to your kind heart but does not do a great deal for my self-esteem. But tell me, what are you doing here?''

"As I told Mr. MacNamara, your mother wished to have a seamstress here full-time. She approached my employer, Mrs. Ferriweather, and Mrs. Ferriweather suggested that I would be suitable for the job.''

"Remind me to thank Mrs. Ferriweather.''

Katie flushed, glancing over her shoulder as she heard the jangle of keys that announced the house-keeper's approach. Mrs. Dixon was not one to tolerate any conversation between servants and the family.

"I have to go.''

She dropped another curtsy and turned to hurry up the stairs. Quentin didn't try to call her back, aware of Mrs. Dixon's chill gaze taking in the meeting from her position down the hall.

He turned away from the stairs. Odd that he should run into that girl here in his own home. He'd felt a surprising twinge of regret at the thought of not seeing her again. He'd been telling nothing but the truth when he said that he'd tried to find where she lived. But one sordid building looked much like another and everything looked different in the broad light of day. She'd probably have sent him off with a flea in his ear, anyway.

Still, it was rather nice to have seen her again. He'd more than half believed that his memories of her were colored by the whiskey he'd consumed. But she was just as pretty as he remembered. The dusting of freckles across her nose would probably have caused his sister to faint dead away with mortification. Ann spent hours applying cucumber cream and never, ever, let the sun touch her face just to prevent any hint of freckles. But somehow, on Katie McBride, they seemed rather charming.

And her hair was just as deep and rich a color as he'd remembered. He still wondered if it could possibly be as soft as it looked.

Quentin shook the thought away. He wasn't likely to find out. But it was pleasant to think of her in the house, to think that they might bump into each other again.

Chapter Three

The hour was late when Katie finally left the Sterlings' Nob Hill residence to make her way home in the darkened streets. Like the fog that rolled in and blanketed the town, tiredness overtook her suddenly. She was grateful when at last she reached home.

She was surprised to see that Colin was there. Seated in their only decent chair—the one Quentin Sterling had sat in, she remembered—he had his feet propped on a packing crate, the newspaper spread open in front of him. He looked up as she came in.

"Hello."

"Hello, Colin." Katie set down the basket she was carrying and slipped off her coat, hanging it on a hook near the door, where the dampness would have a chance to leave it before morning.

"You worked late today," Colin commented, snapping the paper closed and standing up.

"There's so much to do before the wedding." Katie lifted her hat off and hung it next to the coat.

"You've brought work home?" The words were only half a question as his eyes fell on the basket she'd set on the floor.

"Just a bit of embroidery. Oh, Colin, some of the silks are so fine, you could surely pass an entire gown through a wedding band. They must have been spun by fairies, I think."

Colin heard the touch of wistfulness in her voice and felt a rush of guilt. Katie shouldn't be sewing fine gowns for others. She should have someone to sew them for her.

"You've worked late every night this week," he said.

"I know, but the wedding is hardly more than a week away and there's so much left to be done. If I do well with this, perhaps Mrs. Ferriweather will consider me for the position of manager when Miss Lewis marries this summer."

Colin dropped the newspaper and shoved his hands into the pockets of his dark trousers, staring at his sister broodingly. "Is that what you want? To manage a dress shop? I'd not thought you one of these females who yearns for a career."

Katie set the chimney back on the lamp she'd just lit before turning to look at Colin. She knew her brother well enough to hear the tightness in his voice.

"It would mean more money. Some of the girls say that Miss Lewis is getting as much as fifty dollars a month. The extra money would be nice."

"Yes, it would be nice, but is that what you want to do with your life? Do you want to be some dried-up old spinster a few years from now? With nothing on your mind but planning other people's weddings and making dresses for other women?"

Katie cocked her head, trying to judge what had put him in such a temper. "What I want and what I'm likely to get aren't necessarily the same. I'd like a home and family and should I be fortunate enough to meet a man who can give me those things, I'd not turn him away.''

She pushed the image of Quentin Sterling firmly from her mind before continuing. ''But there's no such man in sight and I don't see anything wrong with planning for the future. Speaking of work, aren't you usually gone by now?''

Colin looked as if he wanted to pursue the topic of her job, but after a moment, he shrugged and reached for the crisp linen collar and cuffs that lay on the table. Snapping them into place, he picked up his jacket and drew it on, buttoning it up the front.

''I wanted to be sure that you were safe at home,'' he told her. ''I don't like you walking these streets at night alone, Katie. 'Tisn't safe. I wish you'd let me come for you.''

''Don't be such a fuss, Colin. I'm a grown woman and well able to take care of myself.'' She crossed the room, taking the ends of his tie and looping it neatly, just as she'd so often done. ''What kind of sense would it make for you to travel all that way just to walk me home? And I never know what time I'll be leaving. How would I let you know? Unless you're thinking we should install a telephone?''

Her eyes sparkled with humor at the idea of a telephone in their tiny room. Why, the Sterlings themselves had only installed one a few months ago. She'd seen it sitting there in the tiny cubicle under the stairs. A miracle, it seemed, to think that you could sit at that box and talk with someone all the way across town.

Colin didn't smile in answer to her gentle joke. His

eyes were dark as he looked down at her, his responsibilities lying heavy on him. "It isn't right that you should be working all these hours, Katie. You hardly sleep at all, what with waiting up for me to get back at all hours of the night. Don't try to deny it," he told her when she opened her mouth. "I know you don't sleep till I'm home."

"'Tis a sister's place to worry," she told him lightly, giving a final pat to his tie before stepping back.

"And it's my place to take care of you."

"You do take care of me. You've given me a home."

"Such as it is," he muttered disparagingly.

With a sigh, Katie reached for his hat. There was no talking him out of such moods when they came on him. Their mother used to say it was the Irish in him that brought on these black depressions.

"You'll never guess who I saw today." When he said nothing, she went on, seeking to distract him. "Quentin Sterling himself. You remember I told you that he was staying with his parents. Today is the first day I've seen him."

"Did he see you?"

"Certainly. I haven't become invisible, you know."

"I want you to stay away from him, Katie."

"Don't be foolish, Colin. I'm not likely to see much of him. Not unless he decides to take up mending."

"I mean it, Katie." Colin ignored her attempt to lighten the conversation, his eyes worried. "I've asked about him."

"You've done what?" She turned to look at him,

surprised and a trifle angry. "Why on earth would you make inquiries about him?"

"Because I can see that you're interested in him." He held up one hand to still her protest. "Don't tell me you're not, and I'm not saying that I blame you. But I don't want to see you hurt. He used to be a regular at the Rearing Stallion, though he's not been there for several years. Word has it that he was quite a drinker and a heavy gambler. It wouldn't do to fall for a man like that, Katie, no matter who his family is."

"Colin McBride, do you think I don't have the sense I was born with? I'm not a fool, though you seem to think I am. I know there could be nothing between a man like Quentin Sterling and a woman like me."

She turned away to hide the pain her words brought. It wasn't that she didn't know it was true but it hurt to say it out loud.

"I didn't mean to upset you." Colin put his hands on her shoulders. "I just don't want to see you hurt. You're a fine girl and you're going to meet a fine man one of these days, a man who'll cherish you and care for you the way you deserve."

"I'm not going to be hurt." She leaned against him for a moment. "I know that nothing can come of it. But is it so bad to dream? Just a little?"

Colin's hands tightened on her shoulders, her wistful tone going through him like a knife. "There's nothing wrong with dreaming, Katie. Just don't forget that you have to wake up."

"I SWEAR those stairs get steeper every day."

Katie looked up as the words preceded their

speaker. Edith pushed open the door with her elbow, her eyes on the tray she carried.

"I've told you that I'll come down to get my meals. Mrs. Dixon isn't likely to approve of you bringing them to me up here." Katie set aside the chemise she'd been embroidering and quickly cleared a place for Edith to put the tray. The scent of hot soup and warm rolls drifted upward, causing her stomach to rumble. She'd been so absorbed in her work that she hadn't realized how hungry she was until the food was before her.

"What Mrs. Dixon doesn't know won't hurt her," Edith said pragmatically. "Besides, Mrs. Sterling wouldn't want you to waste time coming down the stairs when you could be sewing."

"Well, I thank you for it. I'd not realized how late it was getting."

"Did you talk to Mrs. Sterling about getting an hour off tomorrow?"

"I did, but I'm not sure I should have. There's so much to be done."

"It's my birthday, Katie. It would be a crime not to celebrate it. And you promised me you'd come to Henri's with me."

"I don't think it's a good idea."

"You're just scared," Edith told her. "It will be fun, you'll see. Henri's is supposed to be the most elegant restaurant, and I had my cousin make the reservations for us. We'll dress in our very finest and go and pretend we're rich."

Katie shook her head but she didn't argue any further. In the short time she'd known Edith Mitchell, she'd learned that arguing did one very little good at all. Edith was the only girl in a family of five boys. This had had two effects. One was that she had learned to fight for what she wanted. The other was that she'd never quite grasped a woman's place in the world.

"Why don't you get Johnny to take you?" Katie asked in a last ditch attempt to get out of going.

"Johnny Kincaid is perfectly content to eat in the kitchen. He'd have no interest in a place like Henri's."

"Quarreled again, have you?" Katie guessed shrewdly.

"Not exactly but he's not the boss of me and it's not likely he ever will be."

"I doubt Johnny would agree with that," Katie said. "When you go out walking with a man on a Sunday afternoon, it's inclined to give them ideas. When Johnny looks at you, it's clear he's got ideas aplenty."

"Then he'll just have to get those ideas out of his head," Edith said mulishly. "I'll not be marrying a man who works in a stable."

"It's respectable work."

"I'm not saying anything against him, but if I marry, it will be a man with some ambition. This is a new century and there's opportunities about for a man who looks for them. Just as soon as I've finished my course at Mrs. Lutmiller's Academy of Typewriting and Essential Office Skills, I'm going to get myself a job in a fine office and I'll have a room in a respectable boarding house. I won't need a man to take care of me. I'll be independent. And I won't be wearing a uniform ever again." She flicked a disdainful hand over the starched white apron that covered her gray skirt.

"Well, I wish you luck. But I'd settle for a good man who wanted a home and family."

"You're too old-fashioned, Katie. Soon women will have the vote, you'll see. And then there won't be anything we can't do."

"Perhaps. But in the meantime, you'd better be getting back to work and I've got to give this dress to Miss Ann's maid so that she can press it." She stood up as Edith lifted the tray.

They left the room together, Edith going down the narrow stairway first, stopping to wait for Katie when they reached the hall.

"Now, you won't back out tomorrow, will you? If you do, you'll break my heart."

Looking at Edith's round, smiling face, Katie found it hard to imagine anything breaking her heart, but she shook her head.

"I won't back out. But if they refuse to let us in, I'll say I told you so."

"Well, well, what have we here? As pretty a pair of doves as a man is likely to find." The two girls turned at the sound of the low, overly intimate voice.

Katie didn't recognize the tall, rather thin man who'd spoken, but from the way Edith stiffened, she guessed that her friend did.

"May I help you, sir?" Edith's tone was neutral, but it wasn't hard to see that the gentleman found no favor with her.

"May you help me? An interesting question." He smiled at Edith before transferring his attention to Katie. Meeting his eyes for a moment, Katie felt a shiver run up her spine. She'd met her share of wolves during her time in the theater and she'd learned how to put them off. But there was something in this man's eyes that made her uneasy. "You're new here, aren't you, my girl? What's your name?"

"Katie, sir." She dropped a curtsy, keeping her eyes on the floor.

"Katie," he purred. "A pretty name for a pretty girl."

Katie jumped as he put out a hand and caught her chin, tilting her face upward. Dislike flashed in her eyes and she made no attempt to hide it. She didn't try to pull back, sensing that it would only encourage his interest.

"Perhaps I'll see if you could be assigned to tend my room, Katie. Would you like that?"

"I'm here to work on gowns for Miss Sterling's wedding, sir. If you'll excuse me, I'm expected elsewhere."

She moved back, forcing his hand to fall as she turned and moved toward the stairs, aware of Edith following her. Behind her, she could feel the man's eyes lingering on her until she was out of sight. She waited until they'd reached the first landing before turning to Edith.

"Who was that?"

"Joseph Landers," Edith told her. "You stay out of his sight. The man's mean clear through. Gives me the shivers, he does. He's Mr. Sterling's nephew and the apple of Mrs. Sterling's eyes."

Catching the sound of Mrs. Dixon's keys, she hurried down the stairs. "Tomorrow at one o'clock. Don't forget. You promised."

Katie continued downward more slowly, one hand absently stroking the fine silk of the dress she carried.

Mr. Sterling's nephew. That meant he was Quentin's cousin. She shivered, remembering the cold gleam in his eyes. Nothing like the warmth of Quentin's smile.

KATIE SLOWED HER PACE as she approached the top of the hill. Henri's sat perched at the very top of a hill overlooking the bay. The restaurant had opened only eight months before and already it was considered one of the city's finest places to dine.

She reached up to make sure her hat was still straight. It was a lovely affair of light blue silk and Tuscan braid, the crown covered with full-blown silk roses, Plauen Venise lace and taffeta ribbons. It had been a gift from her father—to celebrate a successful opening night. As she recalled, the play had closed only two weeks later. Only a very sharp eye would know that it was last year's style.

She'd combed her hair ruthlessly, forcing it up into a neat puff that framed her face—rather prettily, if she did say so herself.

Slowing to a stop, she glanced down to make sure that the rest of her ensemble was in place. The white brilliantine waist she'd made herself, covering the front with rows of tucking and adding dainty embroidery in a shade of blue that just matched the blue silk of her hat. The high neck was finished off with her mother's cameo brooch. The skirt she wore with it was French blue, made of French voile and box-pleated. She'd trimmed it with narrow bands of matching taffeta that circled the bottom of the skirt. From beneath the skirt peeked the toes of a pair of fashionable side-lace shoes.

All in all, she presented a very stylish picture. Certainly, no one looking at her would think that she was a seamstress. Which did nothing to calm the butterflies that had taken up residence in her stomach.

Why had she let Edith talk her into this foolishness? She had stacks of work waiting for her at the Sterlings'. She felt more than a twinge of guilt at the way she'd implied to Mrs. Sterling that it was personal family business that had led to her asking for an hour or two off. If she had any sense, she'd turn around and march right back down the hill she'd so laboriously climbed and go back to work.

But she'd promised Edith, so she wouldn't do the sensible thing. Not just because it was Edith's birthday but because Edith was the first real friend she'd ever had. Oh, she'd met plenty of other girls her age but they'd been from theater families, like herself, and their paths rarely crossed for more than a month or two. By the time she was old enough to consider the matter, she'd grown wary of making friends only to part company. So she'd had plenty of acquaintances, but few real friends.

But in the short time she'd known Edith, she'd come to think of the other girl as a true friend. Edith never failed to make her smile. She was outgoing where Katie was quiet; determined to have a career when all Katie desired was the stability of a home and family. They had little in common but somehow there was a rapport there that Katie had never felt before.

Which was exactly why she was standing here waiting for Edith and her brother to arrive so that they could step through that imposing door and dine among the members of the upper crust.

She heard her name and turned to see Edith puffing

up the hill behind her. From several feet away, Katie could see that Edith was not happy.

"Harry can't come," she announced breathlessly as she drew to a halt beside Katie. "He's got to work, after all."

"Oh, that's too bad. And you were so looking forward to this." Katie could only hope that her voice reflected more regret than she felt. The butterflies began to subside as she realized that, without Edith's brother for an escort, they could hardly go to Henri's. But she'd underestimated her friend's determination.

"I'm still looking forward to it," Edith said, setting her jaw.

"But without Harry…" Katie trailed off, reading Edith's intent. "You can't plan on… Edith, unescorted females don't go into restaurants alone."

"Why not?"

"Why not? Because they don't."

"Well, perhaps it's time they did. Besides, not every establishment feels that way. Perhaps Henri's is progressive."

Eyeing the elegant facade, Katie had a feeling that "progressive" was not likely to be the tone there. Still, the worst that would happen was that they'd be turned away and then Edith would have to give up this whole idea. She followed her friend reluctantly through the wide door, stepping into a foyer paneled in fine mahogany.

Huge mirrors covered one wall and elegant potted palms made graceful accents in the corners. It looked more like the entry to a private home than that of a public establishment.

"May I help you, ladies?" The gentleman who approached them looked exactly as Katie had always pictured an English butler: lean to the point of emaciation with a long sharp nose that fairly quivered as he examined them. They might have been able to fool most eyes but Katie knew beyond the shadow of a doubt that the maître d' knew precisely what their place in society was. His eyes skimmed over her hat and she wouldn't have been surprised to find that he could have told precisely how many months out of fashion it was. His disdainful look brought her chin up, even as color climbed into her cheeks.

Seeing that Edith was uncharacteristically struck dumb, Katie stepped forward. "We'd like a table for two, if you please."

She used precisely the tone Mrs. Sterling would have used and the maître d' blinked, suddenly uncertain of his assessment. On the one hand, his instincts told him that these two young females had no business associating with the exclusive clientele in the dining room. He'd spent years learning to differentiate between real quality and sham. If these two weren't working girls trying to get a glimpse of their betters, he'd eat his hat.

On the other hand, his hat was highly indigestible and there was something in the tone of the small, redheaded one that suggested caution on his part.

"Are you waiting for your escort?" There was a subtle change in his voice, a slightly more placating tone.

Katie arched one brow just as she'd once seen Minnie Maddern Fiske do on stage. "I requested a table for two and as you can see, there are two of us present."

He ceased trying to decide whether they were quality or not. It wasn't worth the risk to just toss them out, as he was almost positive they deserved. He retreated into rules.

"I'm very sorry, madam, but in order to maintain the high standards and reputation for which our establishment is known, we've always made it a policy not to allow unaccompanied females. Now, if you were waiting for an escort..." He let his voice trail off, smiling apologetically.

If it had been up to Katie, she would have nodded and left, grateful to be out without an embarrassing scene. If it had been up to her, she wouldn't have been here in the first place. But Edith had so desperately wanted to dine in an elegant restaurant.

"How very provincial of you," she said, allowing just a touch of a sneer to enter her voice. "I should have known that one couldn't expect the same level of modernity that one would find in New York or Paris."

The maître d' hesitated, still not certain of just whom he was dealing with. If he offended the daughter of one of the Nob Hill families... Still, rules were rules and he could hardly be blamed for following them.

"I am sorry, madam. But I'm afraid that I do not make the rules. I only follow them." He shrugged, looking regretful.

Katie had to restrain a sigh of relief. Edith could hardly say she hadn't tried. Now they could leave and perhaps go to dine somewhere more suitable.

"Miss McBride! What a charming surprise." Katie jumped at the sound of her name. Turning, she saw

Quentin Sterling standing behind them. From the twinkle in his eye, it was obvious that he'd heard at least part of her conversation with the maître d'. She felt a flush start at her toes.

"Mr. Sterling," she managed, keeping her voice level by sheer force of will. Beside her, Edith said nothing, though her pallor hinted that she might simply faint at any moment. She knew as well as Katie did that if Quentin mentioned seeing them here, it would cost them both their positions.

"I couldn't help but overhear a bit of your conversation. Is there a problem, Louis?" He looked over Katie's head at the man who nearly fell over himself trying to reassure him.

"No, certainly not. Not a problem. Just a foolish matter of rules, Mr. Sterling. We have a firm rule forbidding unaccompanied females, as I was just explaining to Miss McBride and her family."

"Well, in that case, it's fortunate that I've arrived, isn't it?" He addressed the question to Katie, who could only manage a weak smile in return. "Naturally, the two of you must dine with me. To tell the truth, I wasn't looking forward to dining alone, so this is really a most fortunate accident."

He didn't wait for Katie to speak but took her hand, drawing her arm through his. Katie felt the touch through the fine silk of her glove and so startling an effect did it have on her nerves that she forgot to worry that he might be able to feel the darning on the fingers of her glove.

Louis led the way through the inner door to the dining room. Katie hardly noted the luxurious thickness of the carpet nor the elegant wallpaper. She nearly forgot about Edith altogether, though a glance across Quentin's body showed her Edith on his other arm. She was vaguely aware of Quentin nodding to one or two acquaintances but he didn't stop to speak.

The table they were shown to sat in front of a wide window with a view of the bay. The weather was clear, and it was easy to see the boats sailing the deep blue waters.

A waiter approached as soon as they were seated. From his deference, it was clear that Quentin was a regular and valued patron here.

"If you'll allow me to order?" Quentin asked his mute companions. While he consulted with the waiter, Katie glanced at Edith, relieved to see that some of the color was coming back into her cheeks. Their eyes met, and Edith gave her a slightly nervous smile.

"I hope you don't mind that I've ordered champagne. I had a feeling that this might be a celebration." Quentin raised his brows in friendly inquiry, looking from one silent girl to the other.

"It's my birthday," Edith got out—the first words she'd spoken since entering the establishment.

"My very best wishes. We must drink a toast."

If Katie hadn't already been charmed by Quentin, she would have been by the end of that luncheon. Not by a word or so much as a glance did he ever indicate that there was anything odd about their presence at Henri's. He treated both of them with the same courtesy he would have shown a woman of his own class.

He chatted with Edith, listening to her plans for a career and agreeing that it was pity women didn't have the vote.

"In Wyoming, where I have my ranch, women were

granted suffrage in 1869. But I have to admit, there are those who claim it was done only to encourage women to move to the territory, to help settle it.''

It was the first Katie had heard of his having a ranch in Wyoming. As he continued, it became clear that he lived there and not with his family as she'd assumed. He was only in San Francisco for his sister's wedding and then he'd be leaving. The thought caused a pang of regret. She would rather have liked to think of his being in the same city at least.

It was probably just as well. Maybe Colin was right. Maybe she was letting her dreams become a little too real. She sighed, toying with her trifle. She'd be better off keeping her sights on getting a better position at Mrs. Ferriweather's than on thinking about a man who would soon be gone and who would no doubt forget her the moment she was out of his sight.

Looking at Katie, Quentin wondered what she was thinking. He'd never known a woman whose thoughts were so well hidden. Her friend, once assured that he wasn't going to fire her on the spot, chattered on nine to the dozen. Katie said very little, so why was it that he found his eyes drawn to her time and again?

He sipped his coffee, listening with half an ear to Edith's arguments as to why women should have the vote. The champagne had loosened her tongue and brought a sparkle to her eyes. She was a pretty girl, with wide brown eyes and soft dark hair, prettier really than Katie when you came right down to it. Katie's features were more piquant than pretty, though the rich auburn of her hair served to take her out of the ordinary.

There was a quality of stillness about her that set

her apart. He already knew all about Edith's brothers and their families, her ambitions. In fact, he felt as if he knew every thought she'd ever had. But Katie said so little. He knew little beyond the fact that she lived with her brother and worked as a seamstress in his mother's home.

When he'd first seen her confronting Louis in the foyer, his first urge had been to come to her rescue. But then she'd put on such queenly airs that even Louis had been set back on his heels. He'd hung back, amused and curious, waiting to see what would happen. When it became clear that she was going to be defeated, he hadn't been able to resist the urge to interfere. It had been worth it just to see Louis scurrying to make up for any rudeness he might have shown. Quentin would have wagered his ranch that Louis was even now trying to discreetly find out just who the McBride family was. The thought amused him no end.

"We really have to be getting back, Edith," Katie said quietly, interrupting his train of thought.

"I know. But this has been truly the best day of my life." Edith sighed, looking around the room as if impressing it in her memory.

"I'd guess there'll be even better days in the future," Quentin assured her. He rose, coming around the table to assist each girl from her chair. Katie hesitated a moment, looking uneasy. "What is it, Miss McBride?"

"I...shouldn't we pay?" she asked quietly.

"They'll put it on my bill," he told her. "No, don't protest. I haven't had such a pleasant meal in weeks and I insist that I be allowed to count the two of you as my guests."

He shepherded them out ahead of him, his hand resting on Katie's lower back. She felt the light touch all through her, making her feel intensely alive. She nodded regally to Louis as they left, not deigning to respond to his overly conciliatory smile. Her eyes slanted up to Quentin's, reading his amusement.

The weather had remained bright and clear, though the fog would no doubt roll in as dusk began to fall. Quentin insisted on calling a hack, though he agreed to drop both girls off a short distance from his parents' home. It was the first time there had been any acknowledgement that anything unusual had occurred.

They rode to Nob Hill in silence. Even Edith seemed to have run out of things to say. When the carriage drew to a halt a block away from the Sterling mansion, she thanked Quentin fervently before tumbling out of the carriage and hurrying up the hill.

Quentin stepped down from the carriage and turned to offer Katie his hand. She set her fingers in his, feeling the strength of his grip as he helped her down. She could still feel it even after he'd released her.

"You were very kind. It meant a lot to Edith."

"I enjoyed seeing Louis set back on his heels. He seems to consider himself the sole guardian of San Francisco society. It was pleasant to see him so thoroughly cowed."

Katie smiled up at him, sharing his amusement, and for a moment, it was possible to forget the chasm that society had placed between them.

She left him there with a murmured goodbye, moving quickly up the hill. Only sheer force of will prevented her from looking back to see if he was watching her.

It was easy enough to slip in by the back stairs. It was only when she reached the second floor that she had to traverse a small portion of the main hallway. The last thing she wanted was for Mrs. Dixon to see her and question her attire. She peered out the doorway, carefully making sure the way was clear before she hurried toward the stairs that led to the third floor and the sanctuary of the sewing room.

"Well, well, well. What have we here? It seems the little dove is a bird of paradise after all." Katie froze at the sound of Joseph Landers's voice. She turned reluctantly to face him as he came out of his room.

"Sir." She curtsied woodenly, keeping her expression blank.

He sauntered toward her, his eyes taking her in from the top of her elegant hat to the tip of her shoe that peeped out from beneath her skirt. When his eyes came back to her face, Katie shivered.

"And what are you all turned out for? Don't tell me, let me guess. You had an assignation with my upright cousin." He saw her stiffen and his grin took on an extra edge of malice. "My room happens to look out on the street and I just happened to be passing by the window and noticed him letting you out of the carriage. Not very gallant of him not to drive you up to the door. And if he's trying to keep you a secret, he really should let you off farther from the house. After all, what if Aunt Sylvie had happened to see what I saw? I don't think she'd be at all amused."

He reached out to lay his fingers on Katie's cheek. She drew back, shivering at the chill that seemed to emanate from his hand.

"Mr. Sterling happened to see me at the bottom of

the hill and he was kind enough to offer me a ride,'' she said with as much calm as she could muster.

''That's Quentin. Always the gallant gentleman.'' The malicious glint in his eyes told her that he didn't believe her story for a minute.

''If there's nothing I can do for you, sir, I really must get back to work.''

''Oh, I can think of any number of things you could do for me, Katie, but none of them proper to suggest right now. Perhaps later?''

She turned away without bothering to curtsy, forcing herself to an even pace as she climbed the stairs. Behind her, she could feel his eyes on her until she was out of sight. It was not a comfortable feeling.

Chapter Four

It was almost a relief when the last few days before the wedding swept the household up in a frenzy of activity. It seemed that there were not enough hours in the day to accomplish everything that had to be done before Miss Sterling could be properly wed. Everything had to be washed and pressed or polished till it gleamed. The huge house bustled with guests and servants, all intent on preparing for the wedding, with occasionally conflicting goals.

At the last minute, Mrs. Sterling decided that her daughter's wedding dress required more alterations. Perhaps she'd noticed that Ann's small figure hadn't quite disappeared in the rows of lace and tucks. Or perhaps she was interested in seeing just how many pounds of lace and beading the girl could carry without collapsing from the weight of it.

Whatever the reason for the decision, Katie was called on to do the work. She marked the position of the new decorations without a word. Not that anyone would have been interested in her opinion. Just as they weren't interested in the fact that she barely had time for the work she'd already been given, let alone this new task.

Carrying the heavy gown upstairs, she muttered to herself, "It already looks like a Christmas tree. Maybe I should just put some candle holders on the shoulders so that Miss Sterling can go to her groom all lit up like a holiday."

The image made her smile and she took the last few steps more quickly, coming to an abrupt halt as she stepped onto the landing and found herself face to face with Joseph Landers. Her smile faded, her hands tightening on the heavy gown. Ever since the luncheon with Quentin, it seemed as if Joseph were everywhere. If she ventured out of the sewing room, she was bound to bump into him. He rarely spoke, but he watched her in a way that reminded her of a cat watching a particularly delectable mouse.

He looked at her for a long, silent moment and then his tongue came out, flicking over his lips. Katie controlled a shudder.

"Well, it looks as if you've quite a lot to do," he said, glancing at the gown draped over her arm, but his eyes lingered on her bosom.

"I've enough to keep me busy." She kept her tone polite, wishing that he weren't blocking her path to the stairway. The stuffy little sewing room, which sometimes seemed such a prison, now looked like a haven.

"You don't like me, do you, little Katie?"

"It isn't my place to have an opinion, Mr. Landers."

Disappointment flickered in his eyes and she knew

that he'd have preferred a more fiery answer. The man actually found the idea that she detested him exciting.

"I'm afraid I may have made a poor impression on you when we first met. The trip from London was quite tiring and I'd only been here a few short days. I'm afraid I was a trifle cranky."

She did not think it possible to dislike him any more than she already did, but she found this ingratiating front even more offensive.

"Tots grow cranky. Adults are merely ill-tempered." Katie regretted her tart answer when she saw interest flare in his eyes, confirming her guess that he preferred hostility to a polite front.

"You like my dear cousin Quentin, don't you? You think he's such a gentleman. Well, perhaps I'll have the chance to show you how much more interesting a real man can be."

Anger flared deep inside her, chasing caution away. She'd been working long hours with too little sleep. Her muscles ached from hunching over her stitching, her head hurt from too many hours spent indoors. She allowed her eyes to flick up and down his lean frame, finally meeting his pale gaze head-on, her contempt plain to read.

"And where do you propose to find a real man to show me?"

It took a moment for the question to sink in. Joseph's face paled, then flushed red. He took a quick step toward her and Katie tensed, ready to fly down the stairs at her back.

He controlled himself with an effort. "You'll regret that, my girl. I'll show you exactly what a real man does with impertinent servants. Soon, my girl. Very soon.''

She met his eyes bravely, refusing to let her fear show. After a frozen moment, he brushed by her. She didn't wait to hear his footsteps fade but hurried into the sewing room, shutting the door behind her and leaning back against it, wishing that there was a key in the lock.

"You've made a mistake, Katie McBride," she whispered. "You've only sparked his interest."

With a shake of her head, she forced the unpleasant scene from her mind. What was done was done and she couldn't change it. Staring at the dress in her hands, she forced herself to concentrate on the task at hand. Only five days till Miss Sterling's wedding and more work than any two women could finish in that time.

Reluctantly, she'd given up going back home, unwilling to spend the time the journey there and back cost. It made more sense to sleep in the tiny room where she did her work. Colin had protested but he'd finally given in, admitting that he'd rather she stayed at the Sterling mansion than attempt the journey home after dark.

The hours and the days before the wedding blurred until Katie couldn't tell one from the other. She'd spent so many hours in this one room that the world outside began to seem a distant fantasy. Mrs. Ferriweather had sent another girl to help her, but she hadn't the skills to do more than simple seam work.

Katie set her to work at the sewing machine and the quiet rhythm of the treadle provided a background for the days. Katie herself did all the fine handwork, applying delicate braids and laces, adding beadwork where Mrs. Sterling thought it appropriate.

By the day before the wedding, there was nothing to be done but row upon row of beading to be applied to the bodice of the wedding gown. Katie sent her assistant back to Mrs. Ferriweather and applied herself to the task, hardly lifting her head from her work.

The monotony of the stitching left too much time for thinking and she found her thoughts turning, as they did far too often, to Quentin Sterling.

"Yes, you *are* a fool, Katie McBride, even setting aside that he's a Sterling—and wealthy in his own right, too—what would he see in you? You're passing attractive but never likely to be a beauty and you've little to recommend you beyond the fact that you're healthy. There's nothing to draw his eyes, even if he weren't who he is and you weren't who you are. But he is and you are and that's the end of that."

The thought was surprisingly depressing, all the more so for having been said out loud. She blinked, clearing her blurred vision as her fingers flew over the bodice. She'd worked into the wee hours the night before and risen with the birds to start again. She'd heard the big old grandfather clock downstairs strike not long ago and she'd counted the stately bongs but she couldn't remember how many there'd been. It must be after noon, and she'd not left this chair all morning.

Maybe that would explain why she felt slightly light-headed and why it seemed so logical that she should be talking to herself. Or perhaps it was that she hadn't eaten. She'd gone down to the kitchen for a cup of tea and a slice of bread and butter that morning.

The kitchen had been abustle with preparations for the wedding dinner.

Edith had promised to bring her noon meal as soon as she could, but she was likely as busy as Katie and had not yet had the time to climb the three flights of stairs from the kitchen. Not that she was hungry. She hadn't felt hungry in a long time. But this odd, hollow feeling in her head might have something to do with a lack of nourishment. It was hard to think of anything beyond the next stitch. She felt as if she'd spent most of her life with a needle in her hand.

She heard the door open but it took several seconds for the sound to register fully. When it did, she slid the needle into the fabric and let the garment fall to her lap. Her fingers had been pinched around a needle for so long that it took a deliberate effort to loosen them.

Looking up, she blinked to focus bleary eyes on her visitor, expecting to see Edith with a tray in her hands. But the figure standing in the doorway was much too large for Edith. Color rushed into her cheeks and she pushed back her hair with shaking fingers, suddenly aware of how unkempt she must appear.

"Mr. Sterling." Her voice was hoarse from lack of use.

"Hello, Katie. No, don't get up." She obeyed his command, uncertain that her legs would hold her.

"What are you doing here?" She realized how blunt the question sounded and struggled to rephrase it, though her brain felt as sluggish as her legs. "I mean, what can I do for you?"

"Nothing." He stepped into the room, leaving the door open for propriety. "The whole house seems to have gone mad with wedding preparations. I'm seeking a small sanctuary. Do you mind?''

When he smiled at her so winningly, she'd not have minded almost anything he chose to do.

"Not at all. I'm afraid there aren't many places to sit."

"Don't worry about it. I've sat more these past few weeks than I have in years. I'm not accustomed to spending so much time in a sitting position, unless I'm in the saddle of a horse. Do you ride, Katie?''

She thought of the one time she'd ridden a horse about Central Park, her leg awkwardly hooked around the saddle while the horse seemed to go wherever he pleased, paying no mind to her futile tugging on the reins.

"I've ridden," she said cautiously.

"In Wyoming, I spend most of my days in the saddle."

"You sound as if you miss it."

"I do. More than I'd thought possible." He crossed the small room to look out the window. Soft rain fell outside, running down the city's famous hills in small rivers, washing the streets clean. There was something melancholy about rain falling on a city. Rain should fall on fields and mountains where the earth could drink it in.

He'd been here too long. Maybe he shouldn't have come in the first place. It had seemed like such a good idea when his mother wrote to tell him of Ann's wedding. Winter still held the ranch in its grip and he'd not been home in nearly three years.

Within him there'd grown a need to find someone to share his life with, someone to celebrate the new calves in spring and curse the early frost in autumn. Someone who could make his simple house into a home. A woman who could work beside him.

But his grandfather had been right when he said that this was the wrong place to find such a woman. Why hadn't it occurred to him that a woman of his own class would never consent to live in the kind of primitive surroundings he could offer?

"Are you thinking of your ranch?" Katie's quiet question made him realize how long he'd been standing there, wrapped in thought.

He turned, smiling in apology. "I do believe I've spent too much time alone. I've forgotten my manners. Yes, I was thinking of my ranch."

"You've not said much about it. Is Wyoming a pretty land?"

"Pretty? No, I don't think you'd call it that. Wild, exciting, stunning perhaps but not pretty. It's too big, too raw for that."

"And you love it for its wildness."

"Yes. I suppose I do. There's something exciting about a land that won't ever be tamed. It's a constant challenge."

"It seems to me that land is the one constant thing. The one thing you can depend on to always be there. A place you can sink roots and grow." She leaned her head back against the chair, her hands idle in her lap, her eye dreamy. Looking at her, Quentin noticed her pallor for the first time. There were dark circles under her eyes.

"You look as if you've not slept."

Katie shrugged, uncomfortable beneath his concerned regard. "I'll sleep tomorrow. There's still much to be done."

"And I'm keeping you from it."

"That's not what I meant."

"But it's the truth. I'll leave you and let you finish your work. I suppose I can find somewhere else to hide from the turmoil. I thank you for the moment's respite you've provided."

Walking down the narrow flight of stairs, Quentin found himself wondering just what had possessed him to seek out Katie McBride. Certainly, if any of his family should discover it, they'd think he'd gone quite mad. Stepping into the second floor hall, he nearly bumped into Edith, who was carrying a tray full of used dishes.

"Mr. Sterling, sir." Edith bobbed an awkward curtsy. Since their luncheon together, she'd not known quite how to treat him.

"Edith. Just the person I was looking for. I'd like you to have cook make up a tray—just some soup and bread. Oh, and one of the cherry tarts we had at lunch. If she argues, tell her it's for me."

"Yes, sir. Do you want it brought to your room?"

"Take it up to Katie. I don't think she's bothered to eat today."

"No, she hasn't. I was going to take her something just as soon as I could."

"Well, do it now and tell anyone who argues that it's on my orders. After all, we both know how important lunch can be." Edith smiled at the reminder of their small adventure.

"Yes, sir. That we do. I'll take a tray up to her right away."

Quentin watched her hurry off before starting toward his grandfather's room. But he'd gone only a step when he heard a most unwelcome voice.

"You're wise to keep the girl's strength up, cousin."

Stiffening, Quentin turned to look at his cousin who slithered out of the reading alcove that had concealed him.

"Joseph."

"Quentin." Joseph mocked his cousin's cold greeting. "I doubt that Aunt Sylvie would approve, you know. Not in her own household. She's one to think that that sort of thing should be handled outside the hallowed doors of domestic bliss."

"I'm afraid I haven't the least idea what you're talking about." Quentin brushed a piece of lint off the sleeve of his pale gray jacket.

"There's no use pretending with me, cousin. I saw that girl get out of your carriage last week and you've just come from visiting her. Rather handy, her having a room all to herself like that. Tell me, is she as fiery as that hair promises?"

The look in Quentin's eyes would have been enough to stop another man but Joseph had never been one to take hints.

"I suggest you not say another word, lest I be forced to knock your teeth through the back of your head." Quentin's tone was quietly icy, leaving no doubts about the sincerity of his threat.

"There's no need to be so touchy, cousin," Joseph protested. "I'm certainly not the sort to tell Aunt Sylvie what's going on under her nose. We men have to stick together, after all. I only thought that perhaps you might consider sharing the bounty, keeping it in the family, as it were.''

Quentin grabbed a fistful of his cousin's shirt, startling a cry from Joseph as he was shoved back against the wall.

"You are to stay away from that girl. In fact, you are to stay away from every female in this household. If I find that you have laid so much as a finger on anyone under this roof, I shall take great pleasure in tearing your sniveling head from your body."

He released his cousin as abruptly as he'd grabbed him. While Joseph was still trying to catch the breath that Quentin's grip had denied him, Quentin drew a snowy handkerchief from the vest pocket of his coat and wiped his hand, the very casualness of the gesture making it more of an insult than if he'd made a production of it. With a last cool glance, he turned and walked away.

"YOU'RE RESTLESS, BOY. Sit down. It's like playing chess with a three-year-old." Tobias's grumpy complaint drew Quentin back to his chair. He sat down and looked at the chess board but he couldn't seem to concentrate. When he stood up again and wandered to the window, Tobias sighed and sat back in his chair, reaching for a cigar.

"What's eating at you?"

"I'm sorry, Grandfather. I don't have the concentration for chess today. Maybe it's all this hullabaloo about the wedding tomorrow. Heavens knows the rest of the house is in an uproar. Ann is in tears because it appears it may rain on her wedding day. She's threatening to put an end to herself if the sun doesn't come out, though how she thinks that will improve the weather, I can't imagine.''

''Foolish chit. She takes after your parents. A couple of nincompoops, from start to finish. You, my boy, are all MacNamara. Don't know how you managed it but, by God, you're all MacNamara.

''You've the spirit and the thirst for new horizons. That's something you never lose, lad, that wondering about what's just over the next mountain. I still wonder. I just don't have the energy to go look anymore.''

''I've found what lies over the next mountain, Grandfather. It's nothing but another mountain and another beyond that. I've had enough of traveling to last me a lifetime and more. I've found what I want. I've a house that looks out on forever and there's not much more a man can ask.''

''Well, then I envy you, my boy. For you've found something I never could. Not even with my Anna. I always had to be seeing what was over the horizon. A sad dance I led her until she finally settled here to wait for me to come back from my roaming. If I'd been able to settle down, perhaps things would have been different. I might have had a son to follow after me. Though I've few regrets. The Lord saw fit to deny me a son, but he gave me you and I've no complaints with that.

''But you take my advice, my boy. You find yourself a good wife, a girl who'll give you plenty of children. A man doesn't have much in this world if he doesn't have a son to follow after him. A strong woman who can stand toe to toe with you and give as good as she gets.''

''You're hardly describing my ideal of a restful

wife, Grandfather,'' Quentin pointed out with a touch of amusement.

"You aren't the sort to want a restful wife. You'd be wishing her to the devil inside a year."

"You could be right. One thing is for certain—I'm not going to find the kind of wife I'm looking for here. It was foolish of me to think I would."

Now why did he think of Katie when he uttered those words?

WHEN THE WEDDING at last occurred, it seemed almost an anticlimax to all the preparations that had gone before. Perhaps Ann's tantrums had reached the right ears, for the sun shone down on her wedding day. A rather weak and uncertain sun to be sure, but sun, nonetheless. She walked down the aisle with all of San Francisco society looking on.

Katie heard the whole story from those of the servants who'd been allowed to stand in the back of the church, entering only after the guests were seated, of course, and exiting before the ceremony was complete. It seemed Miss Ann had been pretty as a picture and the clothes worn by the guests had been fashionable enough to prove the city's claim to being the Paris of the Pacific. All in all, it had been a dazzling spectacle.

Katie had missed it all. She'd set her last stitch just as the sun was peaking over the horizon and had taken the heavily beaded gown down to the bride's room, delivering it into the tender care of her lady's maid. And then she'd stumbled back up the stairs, hardly aware of the subdued bustle around her as the servants began preparations for the big day. She'd barely had the energy to unbutton her shoes before tumbling into bed, and was asleep as her head hit the pillow.

When she woke, it was to discover that the sun was sinking low in the sky. Fog was creeping up from the ocean, drifting through the streets in tattered gray ribbons.

Katie sat up, pushing her hair out of her eyes and yawning widely. Her fingers throbbed and her shoulders ached, the muscles protesting the abuse she'd heaped on them the past few days. Still, the job was done, and well done, if she dared say so herself. Mrs. Ferriweather should be well pleased.

She stretched, aware of a hollow emptiness in her stomach. Food had been of little importance to her lately but it suddenly seemed very appealing. But even more than food, she wanted to be out of this stuffy little room. It seemed as if it had been months since she'd been outside to breathe the fresh air. Even the fog looked appealing. And if she hurried, she might make it home in time to see Colin before he left for the night.

Sliding off the bed, she shook out her dark skirts, grimacing at the wrinkles her daylong nap had pressed in the fabric. Searching among the bedclothes, she found a handful of hairpins, barely enough to control the unruly mass of her hair.

She put on her shoes before shaking her skirts one last time in hopes that a few more wrinkles would disappear. Shrugging, Katie lifted her coat from the chair where she'd laid it what seemed like months ago. She could hear the sounds of laughter drifting up from the first floor.

The bride and groom were to spend the night at the

St. Francis Hotel, barely a year old and one of the most elegant establishments in the city. But if the newlyweds had departed, it sounded as if the guests were lingering, partaking of the Sterlings' hospitality.

Katie had no intention of lingering. All she wanted was home and food, in that order. She yawned again. And sleep. She felt as if she could sleep for a week, or at least the rest of the night. Mrs. Ferriweather would be expecting her at the shop promptly at seven.

She started toward the door, only to fall back, startled, when it was pushed open and a tall figure loomed up out of the darkness.

"What a pleasant greeting, my dear. I wasn't expecting such a welcome." Joseph Landers stepped farther into the room, reaching out to turn on the gas lamp she'd shut off on her way out. Katie backed away, uneasy but not yet frightened.

"If you'll excuse me. I was just on my way out."

"But I won't excuse you." He said it pleasantly enough. There was even a faint smile on his lips, but there was nothing pleasant about the look in his eyes. "You and I have a bit of unfinished business, my dear. Now seems as good a time as any to finish it, don't you think?"

"I don't know what you're talking about." She edged to one side, her eyes flickering to the door. If she could get past him, he'd surely not chase her down the stairs. As if reading her mind, Joseph pushed the door closed with a careless flick of his hand.

"Just to insure that you don't make too hasty a departure. I want to be sure we have plenty of time."

He tugged at the sleeves of his tuxedo, settling them more precisely. With his crisply pleated shirt, low-cut black vest and exquisitely tailored jacket, he looked the epitome of a gentleman.

But there was something in his eyes that made Katie think of a mad dog she'd seen once. There'd been a cold, cruel look in those eyes, as if the only thing that could ease the animal's suffering was to cause suffering in others. She'd pitied the dog, knowing that with the illness upon it, it couldn't help what it had become. Joseph had no such excuse.

"I think perhaps you've had too much to drink. If you'll just let me past, I'll say nothing of this." She was stalling for time, trying to think of some way to get to the door.

"It doesn't matter whether or not you say anything to anyone. Who would believe you—a seamstress, a servant? And even if they believed you, who would care? Are you going to fight me?"

Katie felt her stomach roll. He wanted her to fight. He'd enjoy subduing her. Perhaps, if she didn't struggle, he'd lose interest.

Yet, when he lunged suddenly, catching her arm in a bruising grip, her response was instinctive: her other hand slapped his face. He bit off a curse but didn't loosen his hold, and only dragged her closer despite her struggles.

Three floors below, laughter and music floated upward, a gay tinkling sound at odds with the nearly silent struggle going on in the small room. Even if she'd had the breath to scream, Katie knew it wasn't possible that it would be heard over the noise of the gathering below.

She dragged her nails down the side of his face, feeling a savage satisfaction at his howl of pain. But it was a short-lived victory. A moment later, he swung her around, catching her with an openhanded slap that made the world go gray for one terrifying moment.

Before she'd regained her spinning senses, he'd thrown her across the bed, pinning her down with the weight of his body, catching both her hands in one of his, stretching her arms over her head. Katie arched frantically, but couldn't throw him off.

"Now let's see how high and mighty you are, you little bitch."

Her ears still ringing from the force of his blow, Katie thought she'd never seen anything more evil than the set of his face. He hooked one hand in the high neckline of her dress, bruising her throat as he wrenched at the fabric until the buttons popped loose.

She lay beneath him, bare but for the fragile protection of her chemise. In an instant, that was gone too and he stared down at her naked breasts. For one moment, it was as if time had frozen. Katie stared up at her attacker, the horror of what was happening impossible to absorb.

"Lovely," he murmured, licking his lips. "So pure." He lifted his head to meet her terrified eyes, closing his free hand over one delicate mound. "Am I the first? Of course I am," he answered his own question, his eyes glittering with unholy lust. His fingers tightened with deliberate cruelty until the pain made tears start to her eyes. "I'll make sure that your first experience is a memorable one, little Katie."

The cruel sound of his laughter broke the frozen moment and Katie bucked frantically upward, crazed with the need to have him off her, away from her. She knew that her struggles only excited him more but she couldn't stop. Every fiber of her body revolted against him.

Her frantic struggles seemed to amuse him for he laughed again, the sound drowning out the quiet click of the door opening and then closing again and then the sound of footsteps hurrying down the stairs.

"WELL, ANNIE HAD her big sendoff and Sylvie got to put on her show. Now, maybe we can have a little peace in this house." Tobias lifted the forbidden glass of brandy, sipping it slowly.

Quentin lifted his own glass, settling back deeper into his chair. Two floors below, the guests were still celebrating, though he was willing to wager that few of them could remember just what they were celebrating.

"I hope Ann will be happy."

"As long as his money holds out, she'll be happy. The girl lives to spend."

Quentin would like to have argued with his grandfather's acid opinion but it was too accurate to deny.

"Perhaps she'll change as she matures. She is very young," he offered.

"And perhaps a man can fly to the moon."

"You're in a very cynical mood today, Grandfather."

"Weddings and funerals always make me grumpy. And it was hard to tell which this was. Bunch of nitwits dressed up like penguins. And Annie looked like an advertisement for a furbelow shop."

Despite himself, Quentin chuckled. His short, plump little sister had been completely overwhelmed by her fussy, frilly gown. And the elaborate loops and coils of her hair had completed what the dress had begun. Most of it had obviously been contributed by numerous rats of false hair, tucked in amongst her own locks. At least the overdecorated dress had served to balance the overdone coiffure.

"Heard Mr. Roosevelt is trying to get the Russians and the Japanese to talk peace," Tobias said acidly.

"Well, if anyone can get them to listen, he could. T.R. could get the lion to lie down with the lamb if only he could get them to listen." Quentin smiled, swirling the brandy in his snifter.

"Well, Admiral Togo seems to be leading the Russians a merry chase. If they don't watch out, he'll give them a thorough trouncing and then they'll have to listen."

"I think—"

But what Quentin thought was destined to remain unspoken. The door unceremoniously thrust open and Edith tumbled in, her cap tilted over one eye.

"What the devil?" Quentin rose in automatic response to the air of urgency that spilled into the room along with her. "What is it?"

"It's Katie, sir." She paused, clinging to the door as she tried to catch her breath.

"Katie? What's wrong? Is she injured?" Quentin was halfway across the room.

"It's that Mr. Landers. They were struggling. I came as quick as I could. I didn't know where else to go. Hurry, sir. Please hurry." But she was speaking to empty air. Quentin had already brushed by her. Edith's eyes met Tobias's.

"You did the right thing, girl," he told her. "Katie? That's the little red-haired gal, isn't it?"

"Yes, sir."

"Quentin will take care of it. You should go. She may need a woman's care."

Quentin took the narrow stairs three at a time. By the time he reached the door to the sewing room, he felt rage explode in his chest. His cousin's back was to him as he crouched on the bed and all that was visible of Katie was a length of pale leg and a tangle of gray skirts.

For a moment, he thought he was too late, that Joseph had already accomplished his foul aim. He lunged forward, grasping the other man's shoulder and jerking him backward, tumbling him off the bed. Relief surged through him. Though Katie's dress was torn, Joseph was still fully dressed.

He had only a quick glimpse of Katie, pulling together the front of her bodice, her face white and shocked. Then Joseph came up off the floor, aiming his fist at Quentin's jaw.

It took Katie several seconds to grasp what was happening. At first, all she could absorb was that Joseph was gone. She didn't question how or why. She clutched at her ruined bodice, drawing in great lungfuls of air.

She was vaguely aware that it was Quentin who'd come to her rescue but it didn't seem terribly important. Sitting up, she pushed her skirts down over her legs, noting that her stockings had been torn. She wondered if she'd be able to darn them. Stockings were thirteen cents a pair and the wool to knit them not that much less. She'd have to try to mend these. Now that the wedding was over, she'd have time to tend to such chores.

The fight had moved onto the landing. She heard the harsh sound of a fist striking flesh, and then a solid thud and then silence. Looking at the doorway, she felt nothing. No fear, no curiosity, nothing. It was as if all feeling had been drained away, leaving her numb.

Chapter Five

When Quentin stepped into the room, she stared at him solemnly without saying a word.

"Are you all right?"

"Yes."

She could see that the simple answer nonplussed him but she couldn't offer more. Edith rushed by him, her eyes bright with concern.

"Are you hurt, Katie?"

"No, I don't think so. My dress is ruined, though, and I don't think I'll be able to mend these stockings." She turned her head, a fitful frown creasing her forehead. "If you'll hand me my wrap, I'll be more modestly covered."

Quentin reached out, snagging the cloak from where it had landed across a chair when Joseph ripped it from her. Edith took it from him, her eyes meeting his. This calm wasn't natural. She handed the wrap to Katie, draping it across her shoulders.

"Now, would you look at that. The tie is ruined." Katie tugged at the dangling end of ribbon that had served to hold the cloak together. "I'll have to replace that, too. It seems the mending is never done."

"Are you sure he didn't hurt you, Katie?" That was Edith, her voice gentle.

"Didn't I tell you I was fine?" Katie asked irritably. "My garments have taken more damage than my person."

"Perhaps you should lie down," Quentin suggested.

"I want to go home."

"Perhaps you should see a doctor," Edith said hesitantly.

"I don't need a doctor. I just want to go home." Katie's voice rose, taking on a querulous note.

"All right. We'll take you home," Quentin told her soothingly.

"I don't need an escort," she began, but he interrupted her.

"You're not going home alone."

Her eyes met his for an instant before dropping away. "If you insist."

"I do. Edith, go and tell Graves to bring the carriage around to the side entrance. And say nothing to anyone about this. Not to anyone."

Edith nodded and threw one last worried look at Katie before hurrying from the room. Katie barely seemed to notice her going. She'd wrapped the cloak tightly around her and now clutched it with a grip so tight that Quentin could see the white gleam of bone beneath the skin over her knuckles.

"It won't take Graves more than a moment to bring the carriage around. Are you ready to go now?"

"You needn't act as if you think I'm going to dissolve in a puddle of mush," she told him, her voice lacking the strength to put any real annoyance in the words. "I've told you I'm fit."

But her legs didn't seem to have gotten the message, for when she slid off the bed, her knees threatened to buckle beneath her. Her startled gasp brought Quentin to her side, his hand under her elbow to offer support.

"I'm fine," she insisted but she didn't try to pull away from his grasp.

With both hands clutching her cloak across her torn bodice, she crossed the room with slightly shaky steps. Quentin felt Katie shudder as she paused in the doorway. Joseph was sprawled on the landing, blood oozing from his split lip. He'd regained consciousness and was propped drunkenly against the wall. Hatred flared in his eyes when he saw them.

"Going to finish what I started, cousin?" His sneering words were distorted by his swollen jaw.

Quentin's hand tightened on Katie's arm, feeling the rigidity of her muscles beneath his fingers.

"It's a pity I didn't kill you," he said quietly. "I would suggest that you be gone when I get back, lest I regret my generosity."

The very quietness of his tone made it more threatening than any invective he could have shouted. He turned away, making it clear that Joseph wasn't worth another thought.

Descending the stairs, he could feel fine tremors starting in Katie's arm. The shell that had encased her was cracking, as if seeing her attacker had brought home the reality of what had so nearly happened.

Out of respect for her pride, Quentin waited until they'd reached the foot of the stairs and were out of Joseph's sight before he bent, sweeping her feet out from under her as he lifted her in his arms.

It was a measure of how shaken she was that she

muttered only one incoherent protest before letting her trembling body relax against his broad chest.

With Quentin's arms about her, his long strides carrying her away from the scene of her terror, Katie felt almost safe. But deep inside, she didn't think she'd ever feel truly safe again.

With a soft sigh, she turned her face against the fine wool of Quentin's dinner jacket, shivers wracking her body as reaction set in at last.

Quentin tightened his arms around her. His jaw ached with tension as he carried her down the hall to the servants' stairs. He'd never been able to tolerate someone who used their strength to hurt others. It was a sickness he didn't understand.

But that didn't excuse the fact that he'd let this happen. He'd known what Joseph was like. He'd been a cruel and vicious child and age had not changed him. He'd seen Joseph's interest in Katie. He should have foreseen this possibility.

The carriage was waiting at the side door. Quentin set Katie down, knowing that if he carried her to the carriage, gossip would fly through the house with the speed of a telegraph.

Katie paused, taking a deep breath and drawing herself upright. One hand still clutched tightly at her wrap but the other came up, striving for some sort of order in the tangled mass of her hair. The pins were gone, scattered during the struggle. The best she could do was push it back from her face and smooth some of the wilder curls into place.

Her skin still carried the pallor of shock and there was a hollow look about her eyes; but she looked steadier, more in control.

"I would appreciate the use of the carriage, but there's no need for you to come any farther with me. I'll be fine."

"Edith and I are both coming with you," Quentin said firmly. "I'll have Graves hold the carriage here while I get my coat and hat and tell my grandfather what's happened. I was with him when Edith came to get me," he said in answer to her instinctive protest. "He'll want to know that you're safe."

"There's really no need," Katie said.

"There is a need. I wouldn't feel right about sending you off on your own."

Seeing that there was no dissuading him, Katie acquiesced, lacking the energy to continue the argument. Alone in the carriage for a moment until Edith appeared with her cloak, Katie leaned her head back against the soft cushions, trying to keep her mind a perfect blank. What had so nearly happened simply didn't bear thinking about.

The only conversation during the drive was when Quentin asked Katie for her address, which he passed on to Graves. Katie wondered distantly what the dignified coachman thought of being asked to drive the son of the house, a maid and a seamstress to such a seedy area. There would surely be gossip. It was probably just as well that she wouldn't be returning to the Sterling household.

It seemed as if the journey took only a moment, accustomed as she was to walking the distance. When the coach drew to a halt in front of the worn building she called home, Quentin jumped down first, lowering the steps for her, holding up his hand to assist first her and then Edith.

Standing on the cracked walkway, Katie turned to look up at Quentin. "I thank you for your kindness, Mr. Sterling. If you had not arrived when you did..."

"You don't owe me any thanks, Katie. On the contrary, I owe you an apology. That something like this could occur under my family's roof is appalling."

"There's nothing for you to feel badly about."

"I'm not going to stand here arguing with you. I think you need your own home and your own bed. Will your brother be home?"

"I don't know. There's no need for either of you to come in with me," she protested as Quentin began to shepherd her toward the door.

"Certainly there is. Your brother, if he's at home, will want an explanation, an explanation I certainly owe him. You were under my family's protection when this happened."

"No, really, there's no need." She hadn't planned to tell Colin if she could avoid it. She hadn't wanted to upset him, especially since she'd taken no serious hurt.

"I'd not argue with him, were I you, Katie. I think he has his mind made up," Edith said, slipping her arm about her friend's waist as Quentin opened the door for them, ushering them into the shabby entryway.

With a sigh that was perilously close to a sob, Katie gave in. If the truth were told, she was grateful to have Edith's strong arm about her, grateful for the presence of another woman who could perhaps truly understand the terror of what she'd experienced.

When they arrived at the scarred door of her room, she found her hand was shaking too much to fit the key into the lock. Without a word, Quentin took it from her and unlocked the door.

"Katie!" Colin was home, still in his shirtsleeves, his dark hair only half-combed. He started toward her, only to slow, his smile of welcome fading when he saw that she wasn't alone. "What's wrong?"

"Nothing, really," Katie said quickly. "Just a small incident. Mr. Sterling was kind enough to insist on seeing me home, but it wasn't really anything."

She was talking too quickly. She could hear it, as well as see it in her brother's face. Her words, intended as reassuring, were having the opposite effect as Colin's expression tightened with concern. His eyes skimmed over her, taking in her pallor, the tangled mess of her hair. An end of torn ribbon hung from the neck of her pelisse, which she clutched together in a white-knuckled grip. Even in the fitful light cast by the lamp, it was possible to see the beginnings of a bruise on her cheekbones.

"What happened?" Colin barely got the words out past the tightness in his throat. Katie was all the family he had. If she'd been hurt…

"Nothing, really." But Katie's voice wavered, giving the lie to her words. She pressed her free hand against her mouth as Colin's figure blurred before her.

"Katie!" Colin reached out, his hands on her shoulders drawing her close as a sob broke from her. He couldn't remember the last time he'd seen Katie cry. When she was a small child, she'd cried with each new move, each new set of ties broken. But as she'd grown older, the tears had disappeared, though he could still remember the set look that would come over her face as the train pulled out of each town.

Feeling Colin's strong arms around her, Katie's control dissolved like soap flakes in a washtub. She sobbed into his shoulder, crying out all the fear, crying out the deep exhaustion of the past weeks. But she gave way only for a moment. She drew back almost immediately, wiping at her eyes, her breath shuddering.

"I'm sorry. I don't know what came over me."

"You're exhausted. That's what came over you." Edith bustled forward. "You need some rest, that's all. Let me help you."

It was a measure of Katie's exhaustion that she didn't protest, didn't even think to offer a word of farewell to Quentin. She let Edith lead her away without a word.

Colin waited until the two women had disappeared behind the curtain that set Katie's bed off from the rest of the room before taking a quick step toward Quentin, his eyes fierce.

"What happened?"

Quentin gave him the explanation he demanded in as few words as possible, seeing Colin's eyes darken when he realized what had so nearly happened.

"She wasn't hurt?"

"I believe her hurt was more emotional than physical," Quentin said.

"I should never have let her go out to work," Colin said angrily. He ran his fingers through his already mussed hair. He lifted his jacket from where it had been draped over the back of a chair, jerking it on with quick movements. "I should have insisted that she stay home."

"And watch the two of you starve?" Edith stepped

through the curtains, her eyes flicking up and down Colin in a quick, contemptuous glance. "Katie probably thought that at least one of you should be doing an honest day's labor."

"I beg your pardon?" Colin seemed confused by this attack.

"Well, it's plain to see that you don't hold with working. Just getting out of bed at this hour."

"As a matter of fact, I *have* just gotten out of bed." Colin's temper flared to match hers. "But, contrary to your opinion, Miss—I don't even know who you are."

"Edith Miller, a friend of Katie's and someone concerned for her welfare. She's fallen asleep now. Someone should stay with her tonight, unless you've better things to do, Mr. McBride."

"I'll stay," he said shortly. "And for your information, Miss Miller, though I have only recently risen, it's because I happen to work at night."

"Of course. At the gaming tables, no doubt."

"As a matter of fact, yes."

Quentin broke into what might have become an increasingly vituperative discussion.

"I would guess that Miss McBride would sleep a great deal easier if it were a trifle quieter."

They glared at each other a moment longer before Edith gathered her wrap a bit more firmly about her shoulders and swept by Colin. She paused at the door as Quentin opened it.

"Sleep is the best thing for her now. Tell her I'll be by to see her tomorrow after I've left work."

Colin stared at the door for a moment before turning to look at the curtain that blocked off his sister's bed.

In the quiet, he could hear the occasional half sob that broke the rhythm of her breathing.

QUENTIN WAS FASTENING his cuffs when someone knocked on the door of his room. Glancing up, he bade the person enter, reaching for his jacket as he spoke.

"I've just come to tidy your room, sir. If you'd prefer, I can come back later."

"No, this is fine. I was just leaving." It wasn't until he turned that he realized whom he was talking to. The stilted little voice had failed to ring a bell. "Edith. I didn't realize it was you. Did you see Katie yesterday evening? Is she well?"

"Yes, sir. I saw her." Edith's expression remained wooden, her eyes lowered to the feather duster she was whisking over a narrow table.

"And how is she? Is she rested?"

"A permanent rest is what she'll be getting," Edith said with a touch of acid in her voice.

Quentin had been reaching for his hat and walking stick. He had an appointment at his club this morning. At Edith's words, he turned to look at her, his brows raised in question.

"Permanent rest? Is she ill?"

"Not unless she's sick at the ingratitude that some persons have shown."

"Edith, pray stop talking in riddles," he said shortly. "Is there something wrong with Katie? Did she take some injury from the events of the other day?"

Edith turned to look at him, the duster clutched like a weapon in her fist. "She took an injury, all right. It's just like my brother William has always said. The rich is the rich and they make their own rules. Katie is the one who was injured, so it makes sense that Katie should be the one to be punished.''

''Punished? What *are* you talking about?''

''She was given her walking papers yesterday. Not only from this household, but from her position at the shop.''

''Where did you hear this?''

''From Katie herself. I went to see her last night, just as I'd said I would. Katie told me that Mrs. Ferriweather had let her go yesterday. Seemed she regretted it, but after Katie had made improper advances to one of the wedding guests, she had no choice in the matter. She had to protect the reputation of her shop. So there's poor Katie, booted out of her job and no one to care about it.''

''I care,'' Quentin said quietly, his eyes cold with anger. ''Thank you for telling me this, Edith.''

''Well, Katie wouldn't thank me for it.''

''*I* thank you for it.'' Picking up his walking stick and hat, Quentin left the room, a set look about his jaw that made Edith glad it wasn't she he was planning to talk to.

''EXCUSE ME, MOTHER, but I fail to understand your reason for complaining to Miss McBride's employer about her services. Are you aware that she has been fired?''

''Really, Quentin, what Miss McBride's employer sees fit to do is certainly none of my concern. I simply told her what had occurred.''

Sylvie Sterling twiddled nervously with the elaborate diamond and emerald brooch that decorated the neck of her gray silk dress. There was something about Quentin that made her uneasy, always had, even when he was a child. He'd look at her with those big blue eyes that wanted explanations for things that other people simply accepted. And now, here he was, getting involved in something that was none of his concern. She felt vaguely put upon.

"Let's not argue over semantics, Mother."

"I'm not," she protested indignantly, uncertain of what he meant but sure it didn't sound ladylike. "You know, this is really none of your concern, Quentin. She's only a servant."

Quentin sighed. Staring at his mother's vacant, but still pretty face, he reminded himself that she was not an unkind woman. She just didn't believe in thinking—had, in fact, avoided anything approaching it all her life. A woman's duty was to be pleasant at all times; to dress herself in a manner befitting her husband's position; to maintain, and if possible, advance her position in society.

"Mother, last night Joseph attacked Miss McBride. He could have done her great harm if I hadn't interfered."

"Joseph told me all about the incident. Naturally, I had to tell Mrs. Ferriweather what had occurred. After all, I can't have that kind of thing going on in my house. All our girls are virtuous," she added firmly.

"Katie *is* virtuous," Quentin got out between clenched teeth. "Did you forbid Joseph to return to this house?"

"Certainly not." She was shocked by the idea. "He is a member of our family. The poor boy admitted that perhaps he'd been a trifle naughty but the girl enticed him, Quentin. He was quite embarrassed.''

"Hellfire and damnation!" Quentin shot from his chair, his brows knotting over his eyes as he glared at his mother, who was staring at him in startled shock. "Katie would no more have tried to entice Joseph or any other man than...than you would," he finished irritably, pacing to the window to stare out at the pale sunshine.

"Really, Quentin." His mother drew herself up in her seat, her back rigid with offense. "I don't appreciate your comparing me to that girl. She has no breeding, no background whatsoever. This incident simply proves it. A truly virtuous young woman would never have allowed herself to be put in such a compromising situation. Enticing poor Joseph..." She dabbed at her eyes. "And that's another thing. Do you realize that you nearly broke your cousin's jaw, and knocked out three of his teeth?"

"I'm sorry I didn't wring his worthless neck," Quentin said bluntly, snatching up his cane and hat and striding to the door.

"Quentin." Sylvie's voice rang with alarm. She remembered that look from when he was a boy. That particular set of the jaw had always meant he was about to do something particularly distressing. "Quentin, where are you going?"

He turned in the door, fixing her with cool blue eyes. Instead of answering her question, he asked one of his own. "Did I tell you that I'd come to San Francisco looking for a wife?"

"A wife?" She stared at him, trying to connect this apparently irrelevant statement to their earlier conversation. She half started from her chair as a possible connection struck her. It was too incredible to imagine, but there was that look in his eyes. "A wife? Quentin. You're certainly not— You wouldn't?"

"Yes, Mother, I rather think I would." He grinned wolfishly as she fell back, one hand pressed to her bosom. He set his hat at a jaunty angle before tossing the walking stick in the air, catching it with a wicked grin. "I think Katie McBride might be just the girl I'm looking for."

HE'D ONLY MEANT THE WORDS to startle his mother out of her smug complacency, but as he strode down the street, the idea seemed to grow in his mind. He tried to dismiss it but it persisted. He'd come home to find a wife. Maybe he didn't have to go back to Wyoming without one.

Quentin paused at a street corner, waiting for a trolley to go by before venturing off the sidewalk. He didn't know a great deal about Katie McBride, but she seemed to be a girl of sound good sense. Whatever her background, it surely hadn't been one of ease and luxury. She understood the value of hard work, and heaven knew, ranch life provided plenty of that.

She was attractive and seemed intelligent. Knowing how isolated the ranch was, Quentin understood the importance of a woman he could talk to. Heaven forbid he should find himself sharing a house with a woman, miles from the nearest neighbor, only to discover she hadn't a thought in her brain but fashion. Not to mention that such a girl would have little enough to occupy herself.

No, his grandfather had been right in saying that

he'd not find a suitable wife among the women of his own class. But Katie McBride was another story. She was not ill-bred. In fact, she seemed more refined than some of his sister's flighty friends.

By the time he stopped outside the scarred door of the room Katie shared with her brother, he'd wavered from one side of the fence to the other without coming to any conclusions.

The building was even shabbier than he remembered. His previous visits had been after dark, when the lack of light had helped to mask some of its seedier attributes. He'd narrowly avoided a fall when his shoe caught in the torn carpet and the woodwork showed the scars of too many careless bumps over the years, leaving splinters in the unwary hand.

He lifted his hand to knock on the door, his nose wrinkling at the scent of onions that drifted down the hall.

He forgot about the onions when the door opened. Katie stood in front of him, her eyes widening with surprise when she saw him. Surprise and not much welcome, he acknowledged ruefully. But then he could hardly blame her. The Sterling family was unlikely to be on her list of welcomed guests.

"Hello." He removed his hat, trying a smile on her.

"Hello, Mr. Sterling." Her eyes seemed to soften a bit but she didn't move back from the door.

"How are you feeling?"

"I took no permanent harm. Thanks to you." Did she add the last grudgingly?

"I told you before that you owed me no thanks."

"I'll not argue it with you." Katie shrugged. She turned her head and the light fell more fully on her face, revealing the dark bruises that covered most of one cheek. Quentin's fingers clenched over his hat, creasing the fine felt. The sight of the bruise made him wish he'd taken time to knock out *all* of Joseph's teeth.

"May I come in?"

She hesitated a moment before stepping back to allow him to enter the room. "Colin isn't here."

"I promise to behave with the utmost propriety."

"I know you will." This time he was almost sure she smiled. "May I take your things?"

His hat and cane disposed of, Quentin was suddenly at a loss as to what to say. Looking at Katie, all his indecision faded. She'd make a fine wife, strong, hard working, the sort of a woman to stand beside a man. It wouldn't be a love match but then, after Alice's death, there could certainly be no question of that.

Katie seemed a sensible sort but women could be notional. If she wanted flowery speeches, he couldn't give them to her. And of course, there was always the possibility that there was already a man in her life. It was the first time the thought had occurred to him and it was surprisingly unwelcome. He frowned.

Looking at him, Katie wondered what had caused him to look so fierce all of a sudden. It had been quite a surprise to find him standing in the hallway. She'd not expected to see him again. Not after Mrs. Ferriweather had dismissed her because of complaints his mother had made regarding her moral character.

Oh, Mrs. Ferriweather had been apologetic. She hadn't come right out and said so, but Katie had the feeling that she knew the real truth. But as she'd pointed out, Mrs. Sterling was a wealthy woman and that wealth gave her a certain amount of power. If she stopped patronizing an establishment, many of her friends would follow suit and Mrs. Ferriweather couldn't afford to lose the business.

Katie understood, but it didn't make her any less angry. *She* was the one who'd been attacked and nearly violated. Yet she was the one being treated as if she'd committed a crime. It wasn't fair. But if she'd learned one thing in her twenty years, it was that life was seldom fair.

"May I offer you some tea?" she suggested at last when Quentin showed no sign of speaking.

"No, thank you," he refused, guessing rightly that tea was a luxury likely to be in short supply.

"Would you like to sit?" He seemed so large, looming in the middle of the room. It was a relief when he nodded. He waited until she'd settled herself in a straight-backed chair before taking the remaining seat.

Looking at Katie, he was struck again by the restful air that seemed to drift about her. She sat there now, politely waiting for him to speak, her hands together in her lap. The gown she was wearing was not in the latest fashion, but it was of good quality. The pale green fabric set off the color of her hair so that it seemed to glow with a rich, inner light. There was only the lightest touch of lace at the throat and wrists, just enough to soften the austerity of the simple cut.

"Katie, would you like to see Wyoming?" He heard the question as if it were being asked by someone else.

"I beg your pardon?" She blinked, understandably confused by the seeming irrelevance of his question.

"I've a ranch there," he told her, as if she'd not already known as much. "There's a house. It's not much. Small, rather untidy but there's a pump in the kitchen. Another room could be added, to give us more room.

"The house needs work—curtains, rugs, that sort of thing. I'm afraid I've lived alone too long. A woman's touch would add warmth.

"The land is hard but beautiful. There's snow in winter, sometimes for weeks on end. But in the summer, the grass stretches for miles. There's a small garden, not much but it could be made bigger. The facilities are a little primitive but I could install a water closet this summer."

He stopped, wondering what else he should say. It had suddenly become very important that she come with him. He didn't know why; wasn't even sure he wanted to examine the reasons too closely. He just knew that he didn't want to go back without taking her with him.

She stared at him for a long moment, her eyes searching his face uncertainly.

"Are you looking to hire a housekeeper, Mr. Sterling? For I'd have to be honest and tell you that I think you could do better."

Quentin opened his mouth, shut it again and stared at her. He'd thought he'd made it so clear. Drawing a deep breath, he stood up, thrusting his hands deep in the pockets of his trousers.

"Actually, I was asking you to be my wife."

Chapter Six

In the silence that followed his words, Quentin could hear each separate beat of his heart. Outside, the sharp curse of a driver trying to maneuver his wagon past a carriage broke the stillness, but it didn't seem real.

From the look on Katie's face, he could tell she was as stunned as if he'd suddenly sprouted horns. She'd little enough color to start with but that small amount crept away, leaving her skin the color of fine parchment. Freckles stood out across the bridge of her nose. She stared at him, her eyes wide with shock.

"Did you say—" She broke off, unable to finish the sentence.

"I want you to marry me."

She opened her mouth and closed it again, her eyes dropping to where her hands lay in her lap. Smoothing her palm over the soft fabric of her skirt, she was hardly surprised to see that her fingers where shaking.

"Why?" She looked up at him, her eyes wide. "Why would you want to marry me?"

Quentin sat down again, leaning forward. Now that he'd made up his mind that he wanted her for his wife, he was going to do everything he could to persuade her to his thinking.

"When I came home, it was not only for my sister's wedding. I'm nearly four-and-thirty—time enough for a man to be settling down. When I came home, I had it in mind to find a wife."

"Why me? Surely there are any number of girls who'd be happy to be your wife. More suitable choices."

"I think you are suitable."

"Your family is not likely to agree," she commented dryly.

"It's not my family who'd be marrying. Katie, I need a woman who isn't afraid of hard work. The life I'm offering is not easy, but it can be a good and rewarding one."

Katie smoothed her skirt again, studying the movement as if she could read an answer there. She'd thought that the events of the past few days had left her numb, but when she'd seen Quentin outside the door, she'd known that wasn't quite true. Just the sight of him had been enough to start her pulse beating quicker.

It didn't matter how often she told herself she was being a fool to think of a man so far above her reach, he'd haunted her thoughts. If she was honest with herself, he already held a piece of her heart. If she married him, she didn't doubt that he'd soon hold it all. But to love someone who didn't love her...

"You don't speak of love," she said quietly, looking up.

"No, I don't." Quentin met her eyes squarely. "I'll not lie to you. I know women set great store by marrying for love. But it's my feeling that a marriage can be just as solid if it's based on mutual respect and friendship. And I think we've developed a bit of both, haven't we?''

Katie nodded, her eyes shifting back to her own hands. She wouldn't have called her feelings for him friendship but it was all she was likely to have. Could she marry him, knowing that he might never feel anything more for her than respect and friendship?

''I still don't understand why you're marrying at all,'' she murmured.

''It's not hard to understand. I need a wife. I've had the ranch nearly three years. I've built a strong foundation—cattle, horses and most of the feed to support them. But it's a lonely life. A man begins to crave someone to talk to, someone to share the successes and the failures. I'm building something lasting, Katie, something worth handing on to a son.''

''Then it's a real marriage you have in mind,'' she said half questioningly, the color rising in her cheeks.

''Yes. But I wouldn't rush you, Katie. I have to go back soon. Spring is a busy time and I can't be away from the ranch. There's no time for courting before I leave. But if you married me now, there's no one to say we couldn't do the courting after the marriage. I'd give you time to get to know me, Katie. I'm a patient man, not a boy who needs to rush things.''

He stared at her downbent head, wishing he knew what she was thinking. It was suddenly very important that she say yes. He wanted to take her home with him more than he'd have thought possible just a short time ago.

"Does the thought of a real marriage between us frighten you?" he asked gently.

She shook her head without looking up, her eyes on the restless movements of her hands. "I'm not a child."

"Katie, what happened—what almost happened with my cousin—" He stopped, seeing her tense, her fingers suddenly clenching on a fold of her skirt. "That has nothing to do with what happens between a man and a woman who care about each other," he said at last, trying to choose his words carefully. "I'd never hurt you like that. In fact, for some women, it can be pleasurable."

He stopped again, feeling uncomfortable. This was not the sort of subject a man should be discussing with a woman, not even the woman he'd just asked to marry him—especially not her.

He cleared his throat. "Well, anyway, I wouldn't pressure you into anything," he mumbled.

"Thank you for that." She lifted her head, meeting his eyes directly, though her color was high. "What of your family? They're not likely to be pleased if you marry a seamstress."

"They'll come around."

"You've more optimism than sense, if you don't mind my saying so," she commented.

"Perhaps. Is their reaction so important to you?"

"Not to me. But I know how it feels to lose a family. I'd not like to be the instrument that caused you to lose yours."

"You won't be. We aren't close. It will be their choice, and theirs alone, if they can't accept our marriage."

"That's easy to say now, but will you still feel that way in a year or two?"

"Let me worry about my family." Quentin reached out, catching her restless hands in his. "Katie, we could have a good life together. It's not an easy land, but it is a beautiful one. I'm offering you a home of your own, a place to put down roots that can go deep into the earth."

She caught her breath. How had he known? How had he sensed her deepest need and spoken of it? A home. A place to call her own, a place to build something permanent and lasting. No more moving on. The wail of a train would be nothing more than another sound in the night. It wouldn't have to mean losing everything she'd come to treasure.

She stared at their linked hands. He didn't love her, and she had to accept that he might never love her. But he'd be a good husband, kind and true. And if she bore him strong sons— Well, wasn't there a kind of love that could come out of that?

And if she didn't take this chance, what did she have? She had no job, no reference to take to another employer. She'd be nothing but a burden on her brother, though she knew Colin would never think it.

"Yes." The word was hardly a whisper but she felt Quentin's hands tighten over hers. She lifted her head to look at him. "Yes, I'll marry you."

THE ONLY SOUND was the rhythmic rumble of the train's wheels on the steel track below. Inside the car, no one seemed to have much to say. There was an old man seated near the end of the car, head nodding as he dozed the miles of the journey away.

A few seats away was a young woman who had the look of a teacher about her. From the crown of her fiercely plain hat to the soles of her neatly laced black shoes, everything about her bespoke discipline. Quentin found himself pitying her unknown students.

Aside from the old man and the woman, the car was empty. Except, of course, for their own silent party. Katie sat beside him, staring out the window at the endless miles of prairie that lay beyond. Since boarding the train in Oakland the day before, he didn't think she'd spoken more than fifteen words.

She'd wished him a polite good-night before retiring to the sleeping compartment he'd procured for her. There'd been no mistaking her relief when she realized that he didn't mean to share it with her. Not that he could blame her. After all, he was little more than a stranger to her. She'd spoken an equally polite good-morning upon meeting him in the dining car the next morning. Aside from that, there'd been almost no communication between them.

He supposed he shouldn't be surprised if she was feeling a trifle bewildered by the speed with which her life had changed. Perhaps it would have been wiser to stay in San Francisco a few more days, even a week or two. It would have given everyone a chance to grow accustomed to the new arrangements.

Instead, he'd rushed the marriage through, calling on an old friend of his grandfather's to waive the more time-consuming formalities. Two days after Katie had agreed to marry him, they were standing in front of Judge Reeves, being united in marriage.

The only witnesses had been Katie's brother, who had made his disapproval of the match quite clear;

Edith, who'd served as Katie's only female support; and at the last minute, Quentin's grandfather had shown up, determined to give his support to a marriage that had prostrated Quentin's mother and caused his father to deny that he had a son.

It was, quite possibly, the oddest wedding party San Francisco had seen in a very long time. Tobias MacNamara, one of the wealthiest men in the city; a housemaid; the bride's brother, a dealer in a Barbary Coast Saloon of extremely dubious respectability; the bride herself, a seamstress of Irish decent and a completely unknown background and the groom, scion of one of the most respected families in the state.

Well, the city had always prided itself on the diversity of its culture, a true melting pot. Their wedding certainly proved the truth of that.

Quentin was startled out of his thoughts when he felt a slight nudge to his shoulder. Glancing down, he saw that the motion of the train had lulled Katie to sleep and her head now rested against his sleeve. Moving carefully, he lifted his arm, slipping it around her shoulders and easing her into a more comfortable position.

She settled against him as if she'd slept that way a hundred times. Looking down at her, he felt an odd little tug of his heart. She was too pale. The freckles that were dusted across the bridge of her nose stood out, as did the bruise that still marred her cheek. His hand came up, his finger tracing gently across the bruise.

The foolish extravagance of a hat that she'd worn for the wedding had slipped down over her forehead, making her look rather like a child playing dress-up.

He hadn't realized how small she was until she stood beside him at the altar. The air of calm control with which she surrounded herself had somehow made her seem taller—and older. He reached up to brush back a curling feather that was tickling his nose, frowning slightly.

He hadn't realized until he'd heard Katie answering Judge Reeve's questions that she'd barely reached her twentieth birthday. Not all that young, he supposed. After all, many girls married much younger than that.

She shifted again, her hand falling against his thigh. Quentin sucked in his breath, reaching to move her hand. If he just kept reminding himself of how young she was and of the fact that they hardly knew each other, it might make it easier to forget that they were married.

It had seemed so simple when he was trying to persuade her to marry him. He was a gentleman and certainly in full control of his appetites. Still, there was something very seductive in knowing that the girl who now slept so peacefully on his shoulder was his wife. He found himself wanting to pull the pins from her hair and see it fall about her shoulders.

The long mournful wail of the whistle woke Katie from her nap. She stirred, blinking sleepily. It took her a moment to realize that her head was resting cozily against her husband's shoulder. She jerked upright so quickly that her hat tilted down over her forehead.

"I beg your pardon," she mumbled, her cheeks flushed as she straightened her hat.

"I'd guess you needed the rest," Quentin said lightly, hoping to ease some of the tension that seemed to have sprung up between them with the exchanging of vows. "It's been a rather hectic few days."

"Yes, it has. Is that Laramie we're approaching?"

"Yes." With a sigh, Quentin leaned back. Perhaps it was unreasonable of him to think that they could retain the small friendship he'd thought they'd developed. Maybe friendship wasn't a sound basis for a marriage.

Compared to San Francisco, Laramie was little more than a country village. Compared to the towns they'd been passing through, it was a metropolis. Katie waited at the station while Quentin went to arrange for a wagon. There were supplies to be picked up in town before they started the journey to the ranch.

Katie seated herself on a bench, arranging her skirts about her feet. She fingered the wedding band on her finger, her eyes unconsciously searching for Quentin's tall figure. Her husband. It didn't matter how often she repeated the phrase, she couldn't make it seem real.

A chill breeze swept around the corner of the building and she drew her cloak closer about her shoulders. It was easy to see that the garments she had were not going to be warm enough for her new home. She'd have to see about procuring the fabric for a warmer cloak, possibly some heavier dresses.

She had a few dollars that Colin had pressed in her hand, waving away her protests. He'd not have his sister go to her new home completely penniless. Knowing that it rubbed at his pride that he couldn't give her more, Katie had taken the money. Now it might come in handy to purchase some yard goods.

Her new home. She rolled the phrase over in her mind, liking the sound of it. A real home. A place where she could plant roses beside the door and stay to watch them grow. She'd have much to learn. Living out of a trunk didn't give one the opportunity to learn more than the most basic of housekeeping skills. She could only hope that Quentin would have patience. It would be worth any amount of hard work to have a place to put down roots at last.

Quentin stepped back onto the platform and she rose to greet him, her smile warmer than any he'd seen since the wedding. He smiled back, reaching out to take her hand and tuck it into the crook of his arm.

"I've got the wagon hitched up. If you're not too tired, I'd like to start for home as soon as we've loaded the supplies."

His eagerness to get back to his ranch was palpable, though he was trying hard to conceal it.

"I've no objection," she assured him and was rewarded by the way his smile widened.

Sitting on the wagon seat next to Quentin, Katie took stock of Laramie, aware that Laramie was taking stock of her as well. Quentin drove the wagon at a brisk trot through the center of town, nodding here and there to acquaintances but not stopping to talk.

Her family had trod the boards in many different towns but rarely anywhere west of the Mississippi. Her father had held firm to the belief that civilization stopped at that point, though he'd grudgingly admitted that San Francisco showed signs of embracing true culture.

They'd traveled across the country by train the year she was fifteen and she'd marveled at the great expanse of plains that seemed to go on forever, spreading out from the railroad tracks like a great golden carpet.

The west had seemed a vast emptiness, as if there were nothing between St. Joseph and the Pacific. Now she was to make her home in a portion of that vastness and she looked about curiously.

The sun bathed everything in a crisp clean light, glinting off the windows of the stores. The road was rutted where wagon wheels had dug deep paths in the mud left behind by melting snow. Snow lingered in the shadows near the buildings. Winter had not relinquished its hold entirely.

Delivery wagons clattered along behind horses that looked as if they'd rather have been home in a nice cozy stable. There were carriages and wagons much like the one Quentin drove, though Katie felt that the matched bays pulling their wagon were much the nicest she'd seen.

"Look." Katie followed the direction of Quentin's nod, surprised to see an automobile approaching. "That's Mrs. Morrison's Stanley Steamer," Quentin said as the vehicle approached. "She lives near the edge of town, owns almost as much of Laramie as the Ivinsons and she's been here even longer. She and her husband moved west before the War Between the States and settled on land near the Big Laramie. When he died she moved into town."

He nodded, tipping his hat as the automobile passed their wagon. Mrs. Morrison tipped her head and Katie thought she smiled, but it was difficult to tell beneath the layers of veiling that were draped from the brim of the motorist's hat, shielding her face from the dust and dirt of the road.

"Here we are. This is Lawson's General Store." Quentin drew the team to a halt as he spoke, setting the brake against the wheel. "The ranch is bound to be low on supplies this time of year. We'll stock up here. You can buy the canned goods and whatever else you think we might need."

"But how am I to know what you like? And how many am I buying for? And what can I spend?"

Quentin jumped down from the wagon, looping the reins about the brake before turning to look back up at her.

"I like everything. There are three hands plus the two of us. And I've an account here. You can spend whatever is necessary."

"I must have a budget," Katie protested, looking down at him.

"Why?" he asked simply.

"How am I to know if I'm spending too much?"

"If you spend too much, I'll tell you."

"But—"

"Katie Aileen Sterling, you worry too much. I doubt that you could break the bank just buying supplies."

She returned his smile uncertainly. It was the first time anyone had used her new name since the wedding. He must have seen her middle name on the marriage license and it sounded surprisingly pretty when he said it.

"If I'm spending too much, you'll stop me," she persisted, uneasy with the idea that he was giving her an open purse.

"If you spend too much, I'll beat you thoroughly," he promised lightly. "Now, come down from there before I'm run over in the street."

He set his hands about her waist as she leaned

down. Katie rested her hands on his shoulders, her reticule dangling from her wrist as he lifted her easily from the high seat, making her feel light as a feather.

He didn't release her immediately, though her feet were solidly on the ground. Katie left her hands on his shoulders, her head tilted back to look at his face. There was something in his eyes that brought a touch of warmth to her cheeks.

"You know, it's easy to forget what a little bit of a thing you are," he said after a moment. He smiled, his eyes creasing at the corners in a way that made her heart bump.

"I'm not likely to grow, so if it was an Amazon you wanted, I'm likely to be a disappointment." The sound of her own teasing words amazed her. Suddenly, here in this bright air, Quentin didn't seem so far above her. Here, there was no one to say that she was a seamstress who'd married above her station. She was starting fresh and clean as Mrs. Quentin Sterling, with no one to say she didn't deserve the position.

Quentin laughed, a rich, free sound. His eyes sparkled at her, their color rivaling that of the sky above them. Still smiling, he took her hand and tucked it through his arm as he turned to lead her around the front of the wagon and up the three wooden steps that led to the walkway in front of Lawson's.

Once inside the dim interior, Katie faced a new challenge. She'd never in all her life had to plan on the care and feeding of four men and herself. Just what would they eat? It was a safe bet that their appetites would be hearty, but how much to buy?

She studied labels carefully, trying to look as if she knew what she was about. Quentin didn't seem to feel any uncertainty. He ordered supplies with a lavish hand, never asking the price. When Katie hesitated over the relative merits of canned peaches versus applesauce, he asked for a case of both.

That this was his usual method of purchasing was clear by the way Lawson wrote the order, calling out instruction to the boy who was loading the wagon. Lawson was much more interested in the fact that Quentin had come home with a bride than with anything he was buying.

Katie at last gave in to the tide that was Quentin's method of shopping and ordered what she hoped were essential household goods, closing her eyes to the total she was spending. Dredging up memories of the few times her family had settled into a house and to her mother's housekeeping, she tried to order what was necessary.

Flour, sugar, dried apples, yeast, canned milk, several cases of Uneeda Biscuits, a case of pickles, bearing the Heinz 57 Varieties name, though no one could say just what the 57 varieties were. Jars of Beech-Nut Bacon, which promised to taste just as good as fresh; cartons of oats with the Quaker gentleman on the front.

With memories of a negro woman who'd stayed with the McBride family one summer when her parents had been in a long running play in St. Louis, Katie suggested that it would be cheaper to buy oats in bulk and she could sift out the chaff before cooking it. But Quentin said she'd have better things to do with her time. Besides, he preferred the taste of the packaged sort.

She bought cleaning products, suspecting that a

bachelor's idea of a tidy house was not likely to agree with her ideas. Fels Naptha and Bon-Ami joined the list growing in Mr. Lawson's hand.

"How about some of this?" Quentin suggested, sniffing at a finely wrapped bar of toilet soap. Katie took it from him, studying the picture of two little girls, in fancy dresses, each holding a bunch of violets. Fairy soap, the wrapper said.

"I could make my own soap," she said hesitantly, more memories of Louisa filtering back.

But Quentin shook his head. "I won't have you out stirring a kettle of lye just to save a few pennies. We'll take a case of this, Lawson," he tossed over Katie's shoulder.

She surrendered without protest. If the truth were told, she was relieved, since she had very little idea of how to go about making soap. It seemed that Louisa had spent a great deal of time standing over a great black iron kettle in the backyard, stirring.

With the wagon loaded and the bill paid, they made their farewells to Lawson. Quentin gave Katie a hand to help her into the wagon before stepping up into the seat himself. Releasing the brake, he slapped the reins lightly against the team's back and the heavily laden wagon rolled out of town.

Katie breathed deeply, deciding that she'd never tasted finer air. With Quentin beside her and the whole future opening up in front of her, she was suddenly sure that she'd made the right decision in marrying Quentin Sterling.

It didn't take long to leave the outskirts of Laramie behind. When the last building disappeared behind the wagon, the land opened up before them. The only in-

dication that others had gone before was the road itself, little more than a wide track, full of ruts and
scatterings of gravel.

Katie clung to the side of the wagon as the wheels
bumped in and out of the ruts. At this time of year,
the ground was still damp with melted snow, but she
guessed that in the summer, this must be a dusty ride.

"The road won't be so rough once we get away
from town," Quentin said, easing the horses through
a particularly deep rut. "This close to town, it gets a
lot of travel. Makes the ruts deeper."

Since they'd seen no one else on the road since
leaving town nearly an hour before and there was no
other vehicle as far as the eye could see, which was a
considerable distance, Katie found it hard to apply the
term heavily traveled to the section they were travers-
ing, but she supposed all things were relative.

The land stretched out on either side of them, gray-
green and empty. Though she'd seen much the same
thing from the train, it felt different. Now that she was
actually out beneath the pale blue arch of sky, the
sheer vastness of it was overwhelming. Ahead was a
jagged purple line of mountains. But there didn't seem
to be anything in between.

Just mile after mile of sagebrush. At first, it was
exhilarating. After spending most of her life in towns
where the view was blocked on every side by buildings, to be able to look forever and see nothing was a
pleasure. But as the afternoon wore on, she began to
get the odd sensation that the sky was pressing down
on her. There was simply too much space to absorb.

She was relieved when Quentin turned the team off
the road and down a shallow incline. They stopped in

a little meadow that had been invisible from the road. A stream wound through the center of it, and sagebrush gave way to the first green glow of grass. Snow lingered in the sheltered hollows beneath the trees, thickets of willow. A bird called nearby, a lilting melody that tugged at the heartstrings. Quentin said it was a meadowlark and Katie thought it a lovely name.

The strain of the past week had taken its toll. Even Quentin seemed tired. He spoke little as he unhitched the horses and led them to the stream, letting them drink before picketing them where they could crop at the thin grass.

Katie knelt upstream, splashing cool water on her face, opening the high neckline of her dress so that she could wash the day's dust from her throat. Standing up, she tucked a few strands of wayward hair back into place before shaking out the pale blue skirts of her dress.

Her hat sat in regal splendor on the wagon seat and the setting sun caught her hair, turning it to fire. Glancing up, she caught Quentin's eyes on her. He turned away before she could read his expression, but the intensity of the look lingered with her.

Quentin built a fire, the heat of it welcome as the sun set. Though Katie would have sworn she was too tired to have much appetite, the scent of food changed her mind. After the meal, Quentin washed the tin plates with gravel from the stream bottom.

They retired almost immediately after the meal. Quentin had raised the wagon tongue and spread the wagon sheet over it, creating a sort of tent for Katie's use. She was grateful for the small privacy it offered,

even if it did require some skilled maneuvering to un-
dress in her cramped quarters.

Despite the unfamiliar surroundings Katie fell
asleep promptly, exhaustion winning out over the min-
imal comfort offered by her pallet of blankets spread
over the hard ground. It seemed as if she'd been asleep
only a short while when she was startled awake by a
long, eerie wail. She started up, a blanket clutched to
her chest as the cry sounded again. It was answered
this time, from a distance.

Her heart pounding, she inched over to the opening
of her make-shift tent, sticking her head out cautiously. A full moon hung in the sky, looking close
enough to touch. It cast a clear white light over their
little camp, creating deep shadows where its thin illumination couldn't reach. The fire had burned down
to a bed of coals.

As she watched, she saw Quentin stir from the bedroll he'd laid on the ground, sitting up and reaching
out one long arm to feed a few small sticks into the
fire. The cry came again and Katie couldn't stop the
little gasp that escaped her.

Quentin's head came up, his eyes finding her in the
darkness. "What's wrong?" he asked, pitching his
voice low, though there was no one to hear but the
two of them.

"You didn't mention banshees when you were talking about this land of yours." She tried to keep her
tone light, not wanting to reveal her fear.

"That's not a banshee, though there are those who'd
tell you it's a devil." She caught the gleam of his teeth
as he smiled. The cry came again, ending this time in
a series of yips.

Katie couldn't restrain a gasp, a shiver running through her. There was something so lonely in the sound, like the cry of a lost soul.

"Come here." Quentin held out his hand and she hesitated only a moment before scrambling from her little shelter. Wrapped in a blanket, she was modestly covered, though at the moment modesty was not her first concern. Quentin gestured for her to sit down on his bedroll and he added more wood to the fire until it danced up in a cheerful blaze, banishing some of the shadows.

The wail came again, sounding so close Katie half expected to see the creature standing across the fire from them. Feeling her shiver, Quentin's arm settled over her shoulders, drawing her close.

There was so much comfort in the gesture that Katie forgot to be nervous and let him draw her against his side.

"It's just a coyote, Katie. Like a small wolf, though they don't run in packs. Which is just as well. They manage to do enough damage to the herds as it is. The sheepherders are particularly hard hit when the spring lambs are born. There are those that feel it's no more than they deserve."

"Why would they think that?" Katie asked sleepily. With her eyes on the fire and Quentin's arm about her, not even the sound of another wail could disturb the peace creeping over her.

"A lot of ranchers think sheep destroy the range. They say they graze too deep, making the range unfit for horses or cattle. There's been more than a bit of blood shed over the issue."

"And do you think that way?"

"I think there's room enough for everyone. If you put too many cattle on the range, they'll do as much damage as sheep could ever do. There's a market for wool, and those who want to supply it."

The coyote howled again, farther away this time as if he had decided to continue his serenade elsewhere. "It's a lonesome sound," Katie murmured, feeling her eyelids drifting shut.

"Maybe he's calling for a mate," Quentin said quietly. "Most creatures are lonely without someone to share their life."

There was no response from Katie. She'd fallen fast asleep, her head against his shoulder. It seemed foolish to wake her only to send her back to a cold pallet to fall asleep again. Or so he told himself. The truth was, he rather liked the feel of her nestled so trustingly against him.

She'd braided her hair for the night but a few rebellious tendrils had escaped to curl against her cheeks. She looked very young, very vulnerable and very desirable. He settled her more comfortably. It wasn't going to be as easy as he'd thought to have a wife who wasn't yet a wife.

Chapter Seven

It was barely daylight when Katie woke. But Quentin was already up. She could hear him talking to the horses as he fed them a ration of oats. She sat up, disoriented to find herself sleeping in the open when she'd gone to bed beneath the wagon sheet. It took only a moment to remember the coyote's howling and Quentin's offer of companionship. She must have fallen asleep and he'd let her stay where she was rather than wake her to go back to her own bed. Had he shared this bed with her?

She heard him returning and abandoned the question to scurry to the safety of her little tent. Scrambling into her clothes, she lectured herself on not making more out of last night than was necessary. After all, they *were* married.

When she crawled out of the tent, it was to see Quentin crouched near the fire, feeding sticks into it.

"Good morning." She hoped he'd attribute her breathlessness to the difficulties of dressing on her hands and knees. She wasn't anxious for him to know that it was his appearance that had stolen her breath.

This was a Quentin she'd never seen before. Gone

were the neatly pressed trousers, the perfectly tailored coat and the crisp shirt she'd always seen him wear. In their place was a pair of blue denim pants—jeans, they were called. He wore a thick flannel shirt and a pair of boots with pointed toes that bore little resemblance to the elegant shoes he'd worn in the city. The coat he wore owed little to the fine tailor. It was denim like his pants, lined with sheepskin.

He looked rugged, just like the land. He also looked like a stranger. Even when he glanced up at her and smiled, it was hard to see the polished city gentleman she'd married in the man who crouched so comfortably in front of the fire.

"Good morning." He stood up, dusting his hands off as he approached her. Katie was startled when he bent to kiss her mouth, though she supposed after sharing the intimacy of his bed the night before, it was foolish to be wary of a kiss. But there was nothing to be wary of after all, for it was only a simple kiss, over almost as soon as it had begun.

"Did you sleep well?"

"Yes." She flushed as she said it, remembering just where she'd slept.

"I'm sorry to rush you but it looks like we'll have snow before long." Quentin nodded to the gray northern skies. "I'd like to make the ranch before it gets heavy. If you can manage breakfast, I'll hitch up the team."

He didn't wait for her reply which was just as well. Katie had never cooked over an open fire in her life, but she'd watched Quentin the night before and it hadn't looked too difficult. And it proved to be as simple as it looked. When Quentin came back from hitching the team, she had bacon fried and beans warmed, just as they'd had the night before. Quentin ate without comment, which was as good a compliment as she could have asked for.

By the time they'd finished striking camp, soft flakes of snow had begun to drift down. Katie, who'd always loved the snow, refrained from exclaiming her pleasure. From the frown on Quentin's brow, he didn't share her enjoyment.

It didn't take long for Katie's enthusiasm to fade. The novelty of the drifting flakes soon palled. Quentin didn't try to hurry the team but he kept them at a steady, ground-eating pace. They stopped briefly for a lunch of Uneeda Biscuits and canned ham, washed down with bottles of dark, fizzy Coca Cola, something Katie hadn't noticed him ordering at Lawson's.

When she thought about it, she was surprised to realize how tiring simply sitting on the wagon seat could be. Just the effort of staying in place as the wagon bounced over the rough road was exhausting. There was little conversation. Quentin was concentrating on keeping the team on the road, something that grew increasingly difficult as the snow continued to fall, blurring the landscape so that it was difficult to tell where the road started and the land began.

It was long dark when they at last saw a glimmer of light ahead. The horses had been picking their way slowly over the dark track, finding their way more by instinct than by sight. Katie's head had been nodding for the past half hour and it took an effort to force her eyes open when she heard Quentin's pleased exclamation.

Her first sight of her new home was not very informative. There was a cluster of buildings and she could see the dark lines of fencing. But it was all nothing more than outlines against the snow-covered ground.

The muffled jangle of the harnesses must have announced their arrival because what seemed like a hundred men swarmed out to greet them. It took a moment for Katie's tired brain to sort out the three figures.

"I've brought home my wife," Quentin announced as he jumped down from the wagon. "So I'd suggest you all watch your language."

There were a few confused exclamations and Katie could feel all eyes turning toward her. She made an effort to sit up straight, grateful that the darkness hid the lamentable state of her person.

"We'll save introductions till morning," Quentin said. "The wagon needs unloading. I'll settle my wife at the house and then come back down to help and you can catch me up on all that's happened since I left."

Quentin turned back to the wagon, reaching up to assist Katie. She leaned down to rest her hands on his shoulders but the toe of her shoe caught on an uneven board and she nearly tumbled headfirst into his arms. Quentin caught her as she stumbled, his hands about her waist, lifting her easily from the wagon to set her on the ground.

The men had moved to the back of the wagon to start unloading the supplies. She could hear the snow crunching under their boots as she followed Quentin toward the low building that was to be her home.

In the darkness and with the snow upon the ground, the footing was uncertain and she was glad for the support of Quentin's arm beneath her hand. The second time she stumbled on a hidden rock, Quentin bent, catching her up in his arms, ignoring her mumbled protest. His boots crunched surefootedly over the snow and then there was the sound of the heels striking wood. He pushed open the door, carrying Katie inside.

Though she could see nothing of the room, he seemed to know just where he was going as he carried her through another door and set her down. She waited, her eyes trying to adjust to the darkness. A scrape of a match and the clink of glass and the room was suddenly aglow with light from the lantern Quentin held.

She was standing next to a wide bed. The discovery made her sidle away. If Quentin noticed her movement, he gave no sign.

"Why don't you go right to bed. The place will look better in daylight. Besides, you look ready to fall asleep on your feet."

Katie pushed her hair back, blinking tiredly. It seemed that all she'd done the past few days was sleep and here she was tired again. "What about you?" she asked hesitantly. "It's not right that I should deprive you of your bed."

"I'll bed down on the sofa tonight. There'll be time enough to discuss our living arrangements tomorrow, Katie."

And because she was too tired to argue, and not certain of what she'd say if she did argue, Katie nodded. After all, it wasn't as if she *wanted* to share the bed with him.

After he left, Katie removed her dress, tumbling into bed in her chemise and drawers, asleep as soon as her head hit the pillows.

KATIE WOKE to a clear morning. The clouds that had been building against the mountains had drifted away, leaving nearly two inches of snow behind. Turning over in the soft feather mattress, she stretched, feeling deeply rested for the first time in weeks.

She reached out one hand, studying her wedding ring in the clear morning light. She was a married woman now, with a husband and a home.

She frowned as she sat up, pushing her hair back off her forehead. She wasn't entirely married, not yet. There was more to marriage than putting two names on a piece of paper. Quentin had said he would give her time, but she couldn't expect him to wait forever.

Her eyes darkened as she remembered the feel of Joseph's hands on her body, the look in his eyes. Quentin had said that what had happened had nothing to do with what was meant to happen between a man and a woman. She wanted to believe him.

She shook her head. There was no sense in looking to the past or in looking too far into the future. Right now her biggest concern was to prove—to herself and to Quentin—that he hadn't made a mistake in marrying her. She had to show that she could adapt to this new land, this new life.

She swung her feet over the side of the bed, curling her toes against the chill air. Her trunks sat just inside the doorway. There was a big wardrobe in one corner of the room and a chest of drawers between the pair of windows that looked out onto the mountains, so much closer than she'd expected them to be. The floor was plain wooden planks, smooth and unadorned. There were no curtains at the windows, no rugs on the floor.

Katie felt her spirits rise. She could make a place for herself here. She could learn to cook and to clean. Didn't she remember the old rhyme: Saturday's child works for a living? Well, she'd worked most of her life, first in the theater and then with a needle. Now she had a chance to work at something truly worthwhile.

Sliding off the bed and looking about her, she felt a proprietary interest in everything she saw but most especially in the cobwebs that adorned the corners of the room and the dust that lay on every surface.

She opened her trunk, finding her warmest wool dress. The house was silent and she assumed that Quentin and the mysterious "hands" must be out working. It was after nine o'clock. What time would they want lunch and was she expected to have it ready?

Hurrying into the dress, she pulled on a pair of warm stockings and laced up her shoes. Her hair was given a brisk brushing and pinned back in a simple knot. As ready as she was ever likely to be, she left the safety of the bedroom to explore her new domain.

The house was small, just as Quentin had said. It consisted of the kitchen, a large room that served as parlor, the bedroom she'd awakened in and a small utility room off the kitchen.

The house was solidly built of logs that must have been dragged from the mountains. Rough bark was exposed on the outside but the inside of the house had been covered with smooth planks of pine. The windows were generous, probably more so than was practical when the winter winds howled outside.

There was a wide stone fireplace in the front room as well as a cast-iron stove in the kitchen. Quentin had started fires in both before he left, taking the chill off the air. Katie eyed the kitchen stove warily. She'd have to master its use if she was to learn to cook.

Slipping on her cloak, Katie hurried down the graveled path to the facilities. The air carried an icy bite that threatened more snow, though the sky remained cloudless. Yesterday's snowfall lay in a pristine white blanket over the ground, deceptively cozy in appearance. It was as if winter, faced with the inevitable approach of spring, was reminding the world that it might have a few tricks left up its aging sleeve.

Katie longed to explore her new domain, but she resisted the urge. If she was to have any hope of putting a meal on the table come noontime, she was going to need every minute of the hours till then.

Back in the house, she dug one of her most prized possessions out of her trunk. If Miss Fannie Merritt Farmer couldn't help her, then surely no one could. Carrying the book back into the kitchen, she set it on the big table that dominated one end of the room. There was an enameled pot of coffee on the stove and Katie poured some into a thick mug, grimacing at the blackness of it. Obviously, her new husband liked his coffee very dark.

She was poring over a recipe for a simple dish of beef and vegetables when the back door opened, letting in a wave of chill air. She jumped up, turning around so quickly that she almost tipped over her chair.

"How do, ma'am. I didn't mean to give you a fright." The man who'd entered was about her age, though days in the sun had added years to his face. He removed his hat, running his fingers through a shock of black hair that promptly sprang back into rebellious waves.

"How do you do," Katie said, guessing that this must be one of the men who worked for Quentin.

"Just fine, ma'am. But I'd be doing a sight better if my horse hadn't taken a notion to toss me into a fence."

It was only then that Katie noticed the heavy bandage that wrapped one leg up to the knee.

"Oh, you poor thing. Won't you sit down?"

"Thank you, ma'am, but it ain't like it hurts much. Itches like crazy but it don't hurt no more. Broke it pretty good. Lucky for me that old Tate knows how to set a bone, else I'd have been in trouble for sure. Nearest doctor is near a day's ride away."

"Tate?" Katie questioned as he limped heavily over to the table.

"The foreman, ma'am. He was ramrodding the outfit while the boss was away. Fierce old man but a da— I mean a darn good hand and a fair to middlin' sawbones."

He flushed suddenly, giving away his youth. "I'm Joe, ma'am. Reckon I forgot to introduce myself. It's just that we don't see any womenfolk out here, less it's at a dance. The boss said he was going to find himself a wife but nobody really expected him to do it. 'Specially not one so pretty, if you don't mind my saying so."

Katie smiled as she got another mug down and

poured him a cup of the tarlike substance in the pot. *Quentin had said he was going to find a wife?* Had he actually gone home to San Francisco *looking* to bring back a bride? And if so, how had he come to settle on her? But now was not the time to ponder the question.

"The boss said I was to make myself useful to you, ma'am, seeing as how I'm more or less housebound." Joe looked at her, his dark eyes hopeful. "Is there anything you need doin'?"

Katie's first instinct was to shake her head but then her eyes fell on the huge black stove. If Joe knew the secret to operating it…

"Actually, I was thinking I should start some supper and I've never used a stove quite like this one. If you could show me how to use it?" She gave him her warmest smile, the one she'd seen Maude Adams use in *The Little Minister* on Broadway nearly eight years ago. Though she'd been only a child, she'd recognized the power of that smile. It had brought an audience to its knees and made Miss Adams a star.

It worked its magic on Joe. He blinked at her, his jaw slightly slack. In that moment, if Katie had suggested that he might like to jump off the roof of the barn, he'd have done it without question. The boss had sure enough married himself the closest thing to an angel Joe had ever seen in all his years, few though they were.

"Yes, ma'am," he finally breathed. He stood up, clumping over to the stove, Katie on his heels. "This here is a right fine stove. My ma would'a been proud to have a stove like this back home in Iowa. The boss ordered it from Sears and Roebuck, cost most of thirty dollars."

Katie listened attentively as he showed her how to add wood to the firebox and how to use the damper to control the temperature. If he thought it odd that she seemed to know so little about operating a wood stove, he didn't mention it.

By noon, Katie was more than half convinced that Joe was a gift straight from the Lord. Not only was he companionable, but he was an endless fount of information. He'd been the youngest child of eight, he told her and a sickly boy so he'd spent plenty of time watching his mother work about the kitchen, rather than working outside on the family farm.

If it hadn't been for Joe's knowledge and Miss Farmer's help, Katie didn't think she'd ever have learned how to prepare a meal. The meal she set before Quentin and the other hands was simple but it was edible. The only real failure was the biscuits, which came out rather hard and brittle instead of light and fluffy. Miss Farmer had said to mix them with a light hand but perhaps she hadn't been light enough. Still, the men ate them without complaint, softening them in the juices from the stew she'd made.

There were six hands and by the end of the meal, Katie thought she'd managed to put the right names with the right faces. They all praised her cooking, more than it deserved, she suspected. Quentin lingered after the meal, watching as she carried the dishes to the sink.

"Are you settling in all right?"

"Yes. Joe has been a great help."

"If there's anything you need, just let me know. I can always send one of the men into town."

"Truth to tell, I don't know what I'll need yet."

Katie smiled at him shyly. "I've not much experience at keeping a home by myself."

She didn't have much experience at keeping a home with someone else, either, but there was no reason to tell him that.

Watching her as she moved about the kitchen, Quentin told himself that he had work to do—too much to be lingering here. But there was something very pleasant about watching Katie as she stacked the dishes. Her skirts rustled softly on the floor and he found himself watching the gentle movement of her hips beneath the fabric.

Tendrils of fiery hair had drifted loose over the morning to lie in caressing curls against the back of her neck. He still held the memory of the first time he'd seen her with her hair lying over her shoulders. He'd wanted to bury his fingers in its warmth then and the urge hadn't left him.

He'd had a hard time concentrating on the work this morning. His thoughts had tended to drift back to the house, wondering what Katie was doing, wondering if he should have stayed nearby on this, her first morning.

He'd crept into the bedroom as dawn was slipping over the eastern horizon, finding his clothes as silently as possible. She'd been sleeping as peacefully as a babe, her hair spread across the pillow—his pillow. It had taken considerable willpower to leave the room without giving in to the temptation to wake her with a kiss.

He'd been glad of the cold morning air, thankful when his horse demonstrated his objection to the saddle by trying to throw his master out of it. When he'd married Katie, he hadn't expected her to become so much a part of his thoughts. He'd needed a wife, she'd needed a new beginning. He'd told himself it was a cool, logical decision.

He'd told her that he'd give her all the time she wanted, not thinking that it might be a strain to give her that time. He hadn't expected to want her with such intensity. The sight of her in his bed had sparked images that had lingered in his mind all morning long.

She was his wife. The thought seemed so natural. There'd been a time when he hadn't been able to imagine anyone but Alice in that position, had thought that another woman would seem a usurper. But time changed things.

If Alice had lived, he'd never have ended up on this ranch. They'd have stayed in San Francisco and he'd probably have joined his father's business. They'd have lived a more conventional life. With her death, those plans, that life had also died. And though he'd not have thought it possible at the time, he'd found a full life without her.

"I think we should talk." Katie interrupted his thoughts hesitantly. Quentin shook himself out of his thoughts and looked at her.

"What about? If there's anything you want to change in the house, don't feel you have to ask me first. I suspect the place needs some fixing up."

"The house is lovely," she said, wiping a cloth over the table absently. "I've wanted a real home for so long and this is more than I'd ever hoped for."

"Well." He shifted in his seat, uncomfortable with the gratitude in her voice. The women he'd known

would have thought this the most primitive of surroundings. "What was it you wanted to talk about?"

"It's about the bedroom."

"What about it?"

"You said last night that we'd discuss our...our
sleeping arrangements later."

"It doesn't have to be now, Katie," he said gently,
seeing the flush in her cheeks.

"It seems to me that it's not right that you sleep on
the floor. After all, you are the master of the house
and...my husband."

"I told you I'd give you all the time you need.
We're not going to rush into anything. I've slept in
worse places than the floor, believe me. You'll have
the bedroom to yourself until the time comes that you
feel ready to change things."

"Maybe that time is now," she got out in a low
voice, her eyes on the towel she was restlessly twisting
between her hands. "A marriage should start out as it
means to go on."

"Should it, Katie?" He reached out, catching one
of her hands and tugging her toward him. "Why don't
we see? Come here."

Her eyes flew to his, startled and uneasy. Quentin
felt a twinge of amusement. Did she think he meant
to consummate their marriage right here and now? But
the amusement faded when he felt her hand tremble
in his. She moved closer, stopping when she stood in
front of him, her eyes looking everywhere but at him.
He reached out, catching her about the waist and pulling her down into his lap.

She sat there, as rigid as a board, her eyes focused
on the top button of his shirt.

"You know I'd never hurt you, don't you?"

His gentle voice brought her eyes to his face and she felt some of the fear fade. This was Quentin. "Yes."

She felt a tingling sensation where his hand touched her hair, his fingers finding the pins that held it up, working them loose one by one until her hair tumbled about her shoulders.

"Do you realize we've been married nearly a week and I've yet to kiss my wife properly? Shall we remedy that omission, Katie?"

"Yes." She could hardly get the word out. His fingers had slipped beneath her hair to cup the back of her head, his free hand resting lightly against her cheek.

"Is that all you can say? Yes?" His breath brushed across her mouth as he lowered his head.

"Yes." The word was smothered by his lips. Katie's eyes fell shut, her hands coming up to clutch his shoulders as a warm tingling sensation spread over her.

He kissed her gently at first, teasing her mouth with his. Katie let her mouth soften beneath the warm pressure of the kiss. He'd kissed her at the wedding, but that had been nothing more than a light touching of lips. This was something else altogether.

He drew his head back and her eyelids lifted slowly. Quentin's eyes were dark blue, warm and questioning. He seemed to be looking for something. She couldn't guess at what it was, but she found herself regretting that the kiss had ended so soon.

She was glad when his head dipped again, her hands tightening on his shoulders, her mouth soft and welcoming. But this kiss wasn't like the first. Quentin's mouth was firmer, more demanding, but still not threatening.

She jumped, startled when his tongue came out, tracing the line of her lower lip before slipping beyond to tease at the barrier of her teeth. She quivered, her hands clenching on his shoulders.

"Open your mouth for me, Katie," he murmured against her lips, his hand still cupping her cheek. She obeyed uncertainly and his tongue slid into her mouth, a warm invader. If she could have formed a coherent thought, she would have been astonished at the flush that ran over her body.

His tongue found hers, touching, teasing until she responded, engaging him in a soft duel as old as time. Quentin drew her closer, murmuring encouragingly as Katie relaxed deeper into his embrace.

The hand that had been at her cheek slid down her throat to her shoulder and along her arm. Katie shivered at the light touch of his fingers through the fine wool of her gown. When his hand settled at her waist, she barely noticed it, absorbed in the new sensation his kiss had sent rioting through her body.

But then his palm moved upward to rest against the side of her breast. She stiffened, wrenching her mouth away from his, her hands clenching on his shoulders. For an instant, she was back in that room beneath the eaves, a heavy frame crushing the breath from her, hard, greedy hands at her breasts.

It was an instant only. Then she focused on Quentin's face and the image faded but it was enough to shatter the moment.

"I'm sorry," she apologized before he could say

anything. "I didn't mean... It wasn't you," she stammered at last.

"I know. You've nothing to apologize for."

Quentin stood up, setting her off his lap and turning away, willing his body to forget those moments when she'd responded with such passion. In his mind's eye, he could see the stark terror that had darkened her eyes for that one instant before she'd remembered where she was. He didn't ever want to see that look again.

"I'll do better," she offered, uneasy in the face of his silence.

"Katie." Her name came out on a half laugh. He turned to look at her. "This is not a test that you have to pass or I'll give you a failing mark. You didn't do anything wrong."

"It's a wife's duty—"

"If you finish that sentence, I swear I'll turn you over my knee." She glanced up at the threat, but he was smiling gently. "We're going to spend the rest of our lives together, Katie. There's no need to rush."

His body protested painfully but he ignored the primitive male voice that urged him to pull her back into his arms and erase the memories from her eyes.

"I want to be a good wife," she said, her eyes wide and earnest.

"You *are* a good wife." He brushed his fingers over her cheek. The kitchen was quiet for a moment and then his hand dropped and he spoke briskly, dispelling the introspective mood. "Now, if I'm to be a good husband, I'd best get back to work.

"Put your things in the bedroom. Move whatever you need to to make room. Don't argue," he said firmly, forestalling the protest he could see forming.

"You'll take the bedroom and I'll sleep in the front room. For now."

He picked up his coat and slid it on before settling his hat on. "We've time enough, Katie. It won't be long before we'll share more than a name. I'm sure of that."

He bent to drop a quick kiss on her mouth and then he was gone, letting in a wave of cool air as he left. Katie hurried to the window to watch him walk toward the barn. He swung onto the horse tied waiting at the corral and rode out of the yard. She watched until he disappeared from sight behind the bulk of the barn.

Turning from the window, she stared absently at the stove. "You did better than you knew, Katie," she murmured aloud. "And if he went to San Francisco looking for a wife, then be glad that he found you."

She threw her arms out, a wide grin breaking over her face. She was home, really home for the first time in her life.

Chapter Eight

Dear Katie,

I hope you are happy in your new home. San Francisco does not seem the same without you. Though we hadn't known each other long, I feel as though we had become dear friends. I hope you feel the same.

I was honored that you asked me to be at your wedding. Mr. Sterling seems like a good, kind man. Your brother, Colin, offered to walk me home afterward, since you had to leave immediately for the train station. I was glad to allow him to do so for it gave me the opportunity to apologize for my earlier rudeness to him.

I didn't tell you before you left but it's time I made a clean breast of my sins. That awful night when Mr. Sterling and I brought you home and your brother was there, I made the assumption that he was unemployed and allowing you to be the sole support of your small family.

I feel very badly about having done this, especially as I said some rather harsh things. Fortunately for me, Mr. McBride was quite gracious in forgiving me. I should have realized that your brother could not be other than as honest and hardworking as you are. Though I'm afraid my family would not approve of his current employment.

I am no longer seeing Mr. Johnny Kincaid. You will recall how I said that I would not marry a man who had no ambition. Unfortunately, it became clear that he was quite backward in his thinking. When he found out that I was attending Mrs. Lutmiller's Academy of Typewriting and Essential Office Skills, he was quite disturbed, feeling that a woman's place must always be in the home.

As you know, I do not share these beliefs. You mustn't think, dear Katie, that I am implying any criticism of your dreams. I know that having a home is the most important thing to you. Perhaps, had I spent my formative years traveling, as you and your brother did, I would feel the same.

To me, it is very important that I prove myself in other walks of life before settling into being a wife and mother, which is perhaps the inevitable conclusion to most paths that a woman takes.

I do believe the time is coming when females will not have to make excuses for their desire to have a career, just as men have always had. The new century is but a few years old and it seems a pity to carry on outmoded notions that linger from centuries past. There is much talk of women receiving the right to vote in the near future. I say it's high time that we did so. It's time we had a say in our future.

Pray forgive me. I realize that I have been on my soapbox again, as my brothers call it. I didn't mean to go prattling on so. Please write and tell me how you are going on. Wyoming seems so very far away. Do you miss our fair city?

I didn't mention it to you when last we saw each other, for I didn't want to spoil your wedding day. But now that time has passed, I thought it might interest you to know that the Sterling household was in quite an uproar over your wedding to Mr. Sterling. Perhaps he's already told you about it.

His mother fainted dead away when he told her that he was planning to marry you and his father turned quite purple. I happened to be nearby and heard the shouting match that ensued. You'll be happy to know that your Quentin stayed very cool and told his parents that their opinion held only small interest for him. He said that he was marrying a fine woman and was proud that you'd consented to be his wife.

I was so moved by his sincerity that I was hard-pressed to resist the urge to applaud, which would have been quite indiscreet of me.

I see I've rattled on far too long, as usual. Please write soon and know that I miss you.

Your true friend,
Edith

P.S.: Could you perhaps send me your brother's favorite recipe as he will be coming to dinner a week Thursday. I thought perhaps he might be lonely now that you are gone. As your friend, it seemed the least I could do was to offer him a meal. I knew you would want to know how he goes on.

Katie refolded the letter thoughtfully and slipped it back in the envelope. So, Quentin's parents had been furious that he was to marry her. She wasn't surprised to hear it, though Quentin had never breathed a word to her. All he'd said was that they had some doubts. But when they didn't attend the wedding of their only son, it was not hard to guess that "doubts" was putting it mildly.

Quentin had defended her. It was a pleasant thought, particularly since, lately, his temper had been uncertain at best. She might be innocent, but she was no fool and she had a pretty good idea of what might be making him so testy but she didn't know what to do about it.

The memories of Joseph's attack had faded to the level of an unpleasant dream. Quentin now filled her thoughts. But how could she tell him that? It would seem as if she were asking him to consummate their marriage, a bold move she couldn't bring herself to make.

She sighed, tucking the letter into a drawer, leaning against the dresser for a moment, looking out the window. The last of the snow had melted, turning the yard into a sea of mud that challenged her to keep the floors clean. But she didn't see mud when she looked out the window. She saw rows of young plants, vegetables burgeoning with fruits and flowers turning bright faces to the sun.

It would take more than a few short weeks to make

the dream a reality but she'd made a start on it. Joe had helped her to prepare the vegetable garden and she'd planted rows of peas and greens, tucking in flowers here and there. And beside the front door, she'd had him dig two holes, in which she'd proudly planted American Beauty rosebushes, ordered from a catalog and come all the way from Pennsylvania.

When Quentin had seen them, he'd shaken his head. "They're not likely to survive the first winter, Katie."

She put up her chin. Roses by the door were a part of her dream and she was going to have them. "Then I'll plant them again."

"It's your time," he said, shrugging. "We can give them some protection in the fall and perhaps they'll make it through to spring."

So she had her roses and her house and her garden. The only thing she didn't have was her husband. But surely that would come in time.

Shaking her head, she knelt to open the bottom drawer of the dresser, hoping to find room for a few small mementoes—playbills, her mother's wedding ring, a tassel from the first costume she'd ever worn on stage. That life was behind her, but there were sweet memories there.

The drawer opened only partway before it jammed on something inside. Clicking her tongue in exasperation, Katie worked her hand into the narrow opening and managed to get her fingers on top of the offending object, pressing it down while she pulled the drawer open with the other hand. It came open suddenly, so that she almost tumbled backward.

Brushing her hair back from her eyes, she looked into the drawer, which Quentin seemed to have been using as a catchall for things he couldn't decide what to do with. A broken straight razor, a watch fob with a broken link in the chain, a box of shotgun shells and several other things she couldn't identify.

The item that had caused the problem was a picture frame that had been laid facedown on top of the drawer. Curious, she picked it up and turned it over, expecting perhaps a family portrait.

A lovely young woman looked up at her. She was a year or two older than Katie, with soft skin and wide set eyes that held a sweet expression. She was beautiful, not just in the set of her eyes or the line of her jaw but with an inner beauty that seemed to shine out of her, overcoming the limitations of the camera.

In flowing script across the bottom of the picture was written: So you'll never forget. With love, Your fiancée Alice.

Katie sat on the floor staring at the picture. So Quentin had been engaged to this beautiful young woman. And he'd loved her. She didn't doubt that for a moment. No one could plan to marry this woman and not love her. The thought made her heart ache and her fingers tightened over the silver frame.

"Katie?" Quentin's voice called from the kitchen. She scrambled to her feet, the picture still clutched in her hands. She could hear his boot heels on the floor and she glanced around, looking for someplace to hide the picture. But the open drawer at her feet would have told the tale.

"Katie?" Quentin stepped into the bedroom—the bedroom he so rarely entered when she was present. "Could you—" He broke off when he saw her standing in front of the dresser, the drawer open at her feet, the picture clutched in front of her. From the look that came into his eyes, she knew that he recognized the frame.

"What are you doing?"

"I was just looking for a place to put some things of mine." She heard the guilty note in her voice and stopped, reminding herself that she had nothing to feel guilty about. He hadn't said anything about the drawer being private. In fact, he'd told her to move anything she wanted. She lifted her chin. "I didn't mean to pry."

"I know." He crossed the room and took the picture from her, staring down at it without speaking. Since he didn't seem angry, she ventured the question that burned in her chest.

"Who was she?"

"Alice," he answered, his tone absent. For a moment, it seemed as if he thought that explained everything but then he continued. "Our families were close. We knew each other since childhood. We were engaged."

"Did you love her very much?" She had to ask the question, though she knew the answer could only cause pain.

Quentin nodded slowly, his eyes still on the photograph. "Yes, I did."

The answer settled like hot coal in her chest, making it painful to draw a breath. She hadn't needed the words—the way he was looking at the picture said more than words could ever hope to do.

"What happened?" she asked, needing to know.

"She died," he said simply. "She died and I wished I had died, too."

Perhaps Katie's indrawn breath reminded him who he was talking to. Perhaps it struck him that discussing his fiancée with his wife—albeit in name only—was not proper. Or perhaps the memories were simply too painful to dwell on.

He shook his head suddenly, glancing up at her. Maybe she was a better actress than she'd thought, for he didn't seem to notice anything in her expression.

"It's all a long time ago. I'd forgotten where this picture was." His tone made it clear that the subject was closed. Still carrying the picture, he turned and left. Katie didn't move until she heard the kitchen door close behind him. Then she only moved to the bed to sit down. Vaguely, she wondered what he'd come in for, why he'd called her name.

Alice. Even her name was lovely. The same as President's Roosevelt's daughter. Aristocratic, elegant. A woman from his own world. A woman his family would have welcomed.

Katie wrapped her arms around her stomach as if that could somehow cushion the pain. It didn't matter how often she reminded herself that love had never been part of this marriage bargain she'd made, there was still the small foolish part of her that kept dreaming.

The photograph had left those dreams lying in tatters, had shown her how foolish she was to think that he'd ever come to love her.

KATIE HAD MANAGED to put thoughts of the lovely Alice from her mind by the next morning. She'd received so much from this marriage. It was greedy to want still more. If Quentin never loved her as he'd loved his Alice, then he could still come to care for her and that would be enough. She'd make it enough. Many marriages had far less.

After the supper dishes were done and the kitchen cleared, Katie pumped water into four big kettles and set them on the stove to heat. She and the stove had learned to get along, though not until she'd received several burns for her efforts. She usually made do with a sponge bath but tonight she longed for the comfort of a tub of hot water that she could really immerse herself in.

With the water heating, she pinned her hair up so that it wouldn't get wet. Quentin was down in the barn with one of the mares. He'd told her that he'd be there most of the night. Since it was a first foal, he wanted to wait until it was born.

When the water was steaming hot, she lifted the kettles from the stove, carrying them to the galvanized tub she'd set just close enough to the stove to enjoy the heat. Then she added cold water from the pump, just enough to prevent her scalding herself.

Sliding her wrapper from her shoulders, she dabbled a toe in the water to make sure the temperature was right. With a sigh of pleasure she sat down. The tub was too short to allow her to stretch her legs out, but that didn't matter. With the water lapping at her breasts, she leaned back, making her mind a blank.

She'd listened to the hands talking at dinner. They'd seemed to agree that a storm was brewing, though the clouds building over the mountains looked innocent enough to her. Well, rain would be good for the garden. Without rain, she'd have to haul buckets of water to her little plants. As long as it didn't rain too hard.

She picked up a cloth and set one foot on the edge of the tub, running the cloth over it in a desultory fashion. The warmth of the water was soaking into her bones, making her feel pleasantly lethargic. She tilted her head back, squeezing the cloth out so that water ran down her neck.

And that was how Quentin saw her when he stepped into the kitchen. He froze, feeling the breath stop in his throat. The water lapped around her breasts, half revealing, half concealing, hinting at so much more. Her face was flushed from the heat. She looked warm and languorous, wholly desirable. And wholly out of reach, he reminded himself as she caught sight of him.

She seemed as frozen by shock as he was. She stared at him without speaking for the space of several slow heartbeats, her wide eyes fixed on his face in an expression he couldn't read.

Without a word, he turned on his heel and left, the door banging shut behind him. It was a good thing that he knew the path to the barn like the back of his hand because all he could see was Katie, her skin sweetly flushed from her bath, her hair slipping loose to caress her neck with damp tendrils.

"Damn!" He muttered the curse between gritted teeth. This marriage that wasn't a marriage couldn't go on forever. Something had to give. What worried him was the possibility that what gave might be his sanity.

THE CLOUDS that had looked so innocent the day before had built and darkened until they filled the whole sky to the north in one great gray bank. Katie watched them with a mixture of anticipation and concern. If only the rain wasn't too heavy.

Not that the rain was the main thing on her mind. But it was safer than wondering what Quentin had thought of their encounter the night before.

When she'd looked up and seen him standing there, her heart had seemed to stop. She'd felt no fear as his eyes had slashed over her. The odd quivering sensation in the pit of her stomach hadn't been fear. He'd been so still. She'd waited—for what she wasn't quite sure. For him to stride over and lift her from her bath? And when he'd turned without a word and walked away, she'd felt—what? Disappointment?

She flushed just thinking about it. It wasn't ladylike to think like that. Surely, the lovely Alice would never have had such a thought. She scowled at the gray sky, which seemed to scowl right back.

Alice. The woman had been hovering in the back of her mind ever since she'd found that dratted picture. It wasn't as if she hadn't known that there must have been other women in Quentin's life. And it wasn't that she'd been such a fool as to think that he'd ever give his heart to her.

But it was one thing to know that her marriage was based on practicality and not love, and another thing altogether to find out that he'd once loved deeply, so deeply that he hadn't wanted to continue living without his Alice.

Turning away from the window, she moved to the kitchen table and poked an experimental finger into the bread she'd set to rise earlier. The loaves were ready and she transferred them to the oven, once she'd tested the heat by thrusting her forearm inside. It had taken her much trial and error and more singed arms than she cared to remember before she learned to judge the temperature. She'd buried any number of ruined loaves behind the woodshed, concealing the evidence of her failures before anyone could see them.

But she'd learned. Her bread was as good as any she'd tasted. She wondered if Alice had ever baked a loaf of bread. Katie pushed the oven door shut, exasperated by the way her thoughts kept turning to the other woman. She felt as if she were in competition with the dead girl. But that was foolish.

Alice was dead. Quentin was married to *her* now. No matter how much he'd loved the other woman, his life had gone on. He was building something good and fine here and he'd asked her to be a part of it.

But he'd thought he was asking a woman with some expertise in all the myriad tasks that went with running a home, she reminded herself.

"Well, I've learned, haven't I?" She asked the question of the bowl she was washing, a note of defiance in her tone.

She'd learned but it hadn't been without cost. The singed arms, the burned bread, the garden she hadn't known enough to plant. If it hadn't been for Joe's somewhat bemused help, she'd have revealed her ignorance half a hundred times.

He'd been a help and a companion during her first few weeks on the ranch. While his leg was healing, he'd been limited to tasks near the house and he'd taught her more than he realized. It was Joe who'd shown her how to milk a cow and churn butter, Joe who'd explained how to go about finding the eggs the hens loved to hide.

He'd plowed the garden for her but he hadn't known much more than she did about actually planting it. He had vague memories of his mother planting corn when the oak leaves were as big as a squirrel's ear. But Katie didn't have much idea of the size of a squirrel's ears. Besides, there wasn't an oak in sight. Cottonwoods didn't seem a likely substitute.

Luckily, she'd found a garden manual on Quentin's bookshelf. The title had promised much and it had lived up to its promises: *Growing Food: Being a Manual for the Education and Illumination of Those Who Wish to Provide Healthy Produce for Themselves and their Families. Covering all Aspects of Fruit and Vegetable Culture.*

She'd followed its instruction faithfully and now had a healthy patch of young plants to show for her efforts. It was the one place where she felt she'd been a complete success.

Her cooking was only adequate. The milk cow seemed to despise her, if the fact that she kicked over the bucket every morning was any indication. The chickens showed a certain amount of tolerance but that was because she hadn't yet tried to introduce any of them to the joys of the chopping block. It was still Joe's task to prepare Sunday's chicken dinner for cooking. And Katie found her appetite disappearing every Sunday as she wondered which of the chickens she was cooking.

Quentin left early and worked late. They rarely talked, they still didn't share a bed, so she could hardly say that her marriage was a total success. She couldn't say that she and Quentin knew each other much better now than they had when they got married.

Katie sighed, picking up a linen towel to dry the bowl she'd just washed. Quentin was probably sorry he'd married her and who could blame him? He hadn't looked sorry when he'd seen her in the tub last night. But then he hadn't seemed to have any difficulty turning away, either. Perhaps he had it in mind that, as long as they didn't share a bed, an annulment was possible.

She sighed again, trying to shake the feeling of failure that was creeping over her. Maybe it was just the feeling that a storm was about to break that was making her so tense. If it would just rain, some of the electricity that seemed to crackle in the air would be dissipated.

As if in answer to the thought, thunder cracked, loud enough to rattle the windows. Katie jumped, running to the window as the skies opened with a roar.

In all her life, she'd never seen a storm such as the one she was witnessing now. Rain fell in sheets, a nearly solid wall of water. There'd been no preliminary sprinkles to politely announce the coming deluge. One moment it was not raining and the next it was pouring.

She ran to the back door, throwing it open to step out on the little porch. She was oblivious of the wind that blew her skirts back against her legs as she peered out toward her garden. Would the dry ground be able to absorb the rain or were her small plants going to be washed away? Perhaps if she covered them with some of the bushel baskets she'd seen in the shed...

Her fingers fumbled with the buttons on her shoes. She dropped them onto the porch and stripped her socks off before lifting her skirts up to her knees.

Drawing in a deep breath, she ran into the storm, her bare feet splashing through the puddles already forming in the path.

She was drenched by the time she reached the shed. Stumbling into the dark interior, she found the baskets more by feel than by sight. Lifting a stack of them, she hurried out, pushing the door shut with her foot.

She'd taken only a few steps when she realized that the rain had changed. Where it struck her arms, it stung, like tiny pebbles flung by a careless child. And the ground beneath her feet was rough and cold. Hail. The driving rain had turned to hail. The realization speeded her footsteps. If the rain had posed a threat to her precious garden, the hail surely spelled its doom.

By the time she'd covered the few yards to the garden, the ground was covered by a thin layer of hail-stones. The size of the stones had increased to that of small rocks, striking with force enough to raise welts. But Katie hardly noticed.

She knelt beside the rows, setting baskets over small plants already showing signs of damage. In her mind, it wasn't just a few plants she was trying to save, it was her marriage, maybe her whole life. Since she was a small child, she'd dreamed of sinking roots deep into the soil, building a life. These tiny plants represented that life. They were the newly sprouted seeds of a lifelong dream.

The hail pelted her unprotected head, bruising in their force, but she didn't pause in her efforts.

"What do you think you're doing?" Quentin's bellow startled her into looking up. He loomed over her, seeming tall as a building from where she knelt.

"I'm saving the garden," she told him, without pausing in her efforts.

"Are you crazy?" he asked incredulously. "Katie, it's hailing. You haven't a coat. Or a hat. You don't even have shoes. Come in the house."

He bent to take hold of her arm but she jerked away from him.

"No! Not until I've done what I can." She had to raise her voice to be heard over the storm. As she looked up at him, she saw a hailstone the size of a silver dollar strike the ground between them, while more pelted her head and shoulders.

"Dammit, woman, you'll be hurt. Let the plants be and come inside."

"Not until I've covered as much as I can," she said stubbornly.

"Now." She tried to pull back as he took her arm but this time, he didn't release her. He drew her to her feet, glaring at her from under the brim of his hat.

"Let me go," she demanded, trying to twist her arm away.

"Let the damn plants take care of themselves," he all but shouted.

"I won't."

A bolt of lightning speared down, striking the earth so near them that the air seemed electrified by the power it held. Thunder crashed in a deafening crescendo. Katie glared at Quentin, no sign of give in her pose.

"You will," Quentin said calmly. He stepped forward, bending to catch her under the knees and shoulders. There was time for only a gasp as he scooped her up against his chest and strode toward the house.

Katie made one convulsive attempt to escape and then held still, knowing he wasn't going to let her go.

There was another slash of lightning and Quentin's strides lengthened, his boot hitting the bottom step as the thunder roared. The door slammed shut behind them, shutting the storm out.

The kitchen was warm, filled with the rich scent of baking bread. He set her on her feet in the middle of the floor. Her hair hung down her back in a thick, wet braid. Her dress was soaking wet, the light wool clinging to her in a way that might have struck her as immodest at another time. But modesty wasn't on her mind at the moment.

"Are you crazy?" Quentin demanded, glaring at her, his eyes dark and stormy under the shadow of his hat. "That's hail. We can get hailstones the size of a man's fist in one of these storms. You were out there without a coat, without a hat, without shoes."

"I had to cover the plants," she said stubbornly, raising her chin a notch. For the first time since they'd met, she wasn't conscious of the fact that he came from a level of society she couldn't normally approach, or of the fact that he could have married any number of girls from his own class, or of the fact that he'd brought so much more to this marriage than she had.

"Look at your arm," he said angrily, grabbing her hand and pushing the sleeve up to show her the reddened skin. "And you're soaking wet. You could catch pneumonia. And the nearest doctor is nearly a day's ride away."

"Don't worry. If I catch pneumonia, I'll try to die peacefully without disturbing you by asking you to send for the doctor.'' She hardly knew what she was saying. Tears blurred his tall figure. All the tension of trying to learn a lifetime of things in a few short weeks, of pretending to be something she wasn't, had worn away her control.

"I didn't say it would disturb me to send for the doctor,'' Quentin protested, trying to understand how the subject had changed. "Katie, they're just plants.''

"It was the one thing I'd done right,'' she lashed out, wiping angrily at the tears on her cheeks. "The cow hates me and I can't kill a chicken and my cooking is hardly worth mentioning, but those plants were growing.''

"Katie.'' Quentin's voice softened when he saw her distress. He reached for her shoulders but she twitched them away.

"I don't need your pity,'' she snapped, her chin coming up. "You married me out of pity. I knew that. You went to San Francisco to look for a wife and you felt sorry for me. You brought me here and found that pity wasn't enough to build a marriage on. Well, it's not enough for me, either. I may not come from a Nob Hill family but the McBrides have as much to be proud of as the Sterlings any day. I don't need your pity.''

"Katie.'' He reached out, ignoring her attempt to pull away from him. She was rigid in his grasp as he drew her close. She stared at one of the buttons on his coat, willing back the tears that threatened to become a deluge to rival the one outside.

"I didn't marry you out of pity.'' His hand slipped under her chin, tilting her face up to his. Katie kept her eyes lowered, refusing to meet his eyes. "I married you because I thought we could make a good marriage together. Only a fool would marry for pity.''

His words brought her eyes to his and she could see nothing but honesty in them. ''Then why haven't you…''

She broke off, feeling her cheeks flush as she looked away from him. But Quentin understood her meaning.

''I said I'd give you time.'' He let his hand slip from her chin to rest along the side of her neck, his thumb brushing her ear. ''I didn't want to rush you, Katie.''

''You're not rushing me,'' she said, her voice hardly more than a whisper, her cheeks burning at her own boldness.

He pulled her a step closer so that there was hardly a whisper between them. Katie closed her eyes, afraid of what he might see, afraid her eyes might tell him things she wasn't ready to admit, even to herself.

''Look at me, Katie.'' His breath brushed across her forehead and her lashes lifted slowly. She could only guess at what he saw in her eyes, but the look in his sent a shiver down her spine. Quentin felt the small movement. ''Are you afraid of me, Katie?''

Afraid of him? No, she couldn't in truth say that she feared him. It was more that she feared what he made her feel. This shivery awareness was new to her. But that wasn't what he was asking. She shook her head slowly.

''I know you'd not willingly hurt me,'' she answered at last.

''Willingly?'' He questioned the qualifying word. ''Do you think I'd hurt you unwillingly?''

The fingers at her neck moved back to comb

through the damp braid of her hair, separating it, spreading it across her shoulders.

"I can't say. I'm no gypsy to be looking into the future."

His hands moved again until he cupped her face between his palms. Katie felt the roughness of callused skin against the softness of her cheeks. She felt his touch deep inside, reaching to the very core of her and stirring new feelings.

"Katie Aileen Sterling, I promise I'll never knowingly cause you pain. Do you believe that?"

"Yes." The word breathed out, her eyes on his.

"We've a marriage that isn't a marriage. It seems to me it's time we did something about it. Do you trust me?"

The hands she set against his chest trembled and her voice was little more than a whisper, but her eyes were steady on his as she answered.

"With my life."

This kiss was different from the other they'd shared. It held more demand, more hunger, more need. It was the need she responded to, opening her lips to him, her tongue entwining with his as she sank against his chest.

After a moment, Quentin lifted his head. He looked down into her eyes, feeling his stomach tighten at the innocent sensuality of her gaze. He wanted her. He couldn't remember the last time he'd wanted something so badly. It wasn't just a sexual need, it was a deep visceral hunger that only she could satisfy.

She gasped as he bent, scooping her up in his arms as if she weighed no more than a feather.

"I'm wet."

"I'll help you get dry," he said huskily, his mouth coming down on hers as he carried her into the bedroom.

Outside, the hail had turned to rain. The worst of the storm had passed overhead, leaving an occasional rumble of thunder to growl in the distance. The clouds blocked out the sunlight, leaving the bedroom dim.

Quentin set Katie down next to the bed. He undressed her slowly, his eyes never leaving hers. In the back of her mind was the thought that this was a sinful thing to be doing in the middle of the day. But it didn't feel sinful. It felt right. For the first time, she didn't feel like an unwelcome visitor in this room.

She stood before him at last, clad in nothing but thin cotton knickers and lace-trimmed chemise. Her bare toes curled against the floor uncertainly. Was he disappointed in her? She wasn't tall, nor was her figure overly rounded. Had he hoped for more?

But there was no disappointment in Quentin's eyes, none in his touch as he tugged loose the ribbon bow at the top of her chemise. The tiny pearl buttons fell open beneath his touch and Katie gasped as his hand slid inside to cup her breast. She'd never dreamed a simple touch could start such a fire raging inside her.

She felt a deep sense of loss when his hand left her, but it was only so he could strip off his coat, dropping it to the floor. His shirt soon followed. Her vision was filled with the width of his chest. A thick mat of golden-brown hair covered the taut muscles, tapering to a thin line that disappeared into the waistband of his jeans.

She jerked her eyes up, her cheeks flushing at the glimpse she'd had of his arousal. The flush deepened when Quentin's hands went to the buttons of his pants. She stood there, rigid, looking anywhere but at him as he unbuttoned the jeans.

But he didn't take them off immediately. Instead, he reached for her hands, setting her palms against his chest and holding them there until he felt her relax. Slowly, she moved her fingers, feeling the springy mat of hair curl against her hands. Quentin held his breath as her palms brushed over him. The innocent exploration was somehow more erotic than the practiced touch of the most experienced courtesan.

Burying his fingers in her hair, he tilted her head back, catching her mouth with his. Katie felt her head spin as he pulled her close, slipping the chemise from her shoulders so that her breasts pressed boldly against the warm skin of his chest.

Nothing could have prepared her for the feelings that flowed through her. She'd thought of this moment since the wedding. She'd wanted Quentin's touch and dreaded it. In the back of her mind, she'd remembered Joseph's hands, hard and hurting, remembered the feeling of fear and humiliation that had accompanied his touch.

But nothing in Quentin's touch reminded her of Joseph. His hands caressed, they didn't hurt. In a matter of minutes, she could think of nothing but the warm pleasure washing over her.

When Quentin lifted her onto the bed and kicked off his jeans before following her down into the feather mattress, Katie opened her arms to him. This was her husband.

This was the man she loved with all her heart.

Chapter Nine

Katie came awake slowly. Her sleep had been light but restful. Outside, the rain had slowed to a gentle shower, the moisture sinking into the grateful earth rather than battering it.

She stirred in the big bed, aware of a feeling of fulfillment she'd never had before. Without opening her eyes, she shifted one foot, cautiously seeking. She wasn't sure whether she felt relief or disappointment when she found she was alone. Opening her eyes, she stared up at the ceiling, seeing the same wide beams and smooth planks she'd seen for the past few weeks.

But they didn't look the same. Everything looked new and different, just as she felt new and different. She sat up, wrapping her arms around her shins and resting her chin on her updrawn knees.

She was really and truly a married woman now. Odd, how something she'd regarded with a mixture of fear and fascination should turn out to feel so natural. Wonderful actually, she admitted to herself, feeling the color flood her face as she remembered the response she'd given so readily.

There was a muffled thud from the direction of the

kitchen and Katie swung her legs off the bed. She'd thought Quentin was gone and she'd been half sorry, half relieved. She wasn't sure she was ready to face him again quite yet. On the other hand, she couldn't hide in the bedroom, particularly not dressed as she was—or as she wasn't.

She dressed hastily, muttering over uncooperative buttons, terrified that Quentin would walk in at any moment. They might have made their marriage a real one at last but it was going to take her a while to get used to the idea of sharing a room with him.

Another thud made her decide against trying to pin her hair up. She had allowed it to dry without combing it, and it now fell in a thick mass of curls to her waist. A glimpse in the mirror told her that she looked like a wild woman. She tied the unruly mass back with a wide ribbon.

Katie approached the kitchen warily. There was an odd smell in the air, slightly harsh as if something were burning.

"My bread!" She entered the kitchen in a rush, giving a moan of despair when she saw the loaves sitting in the middle of the big table, their crusts nearly black.

Quentin turned from the stove, the last pan in his hand. At another time, she might have found the incongruous sight of him—shirtless and barefoot, a towel wrapped around his hand to protect him from the hot pan—more than a little appealing. But at the moment, all she could think of was that she'd failed yet again.

"I smelled them burning," he said as he turned the

last loaf out of the pans and onto the table. "It's too bad I didn't smell them a bit sooner."

"I followed the steps so carefully this time," she said sadly.

"It was my fault for distracting you."

At that, she glanced at him, the ruined bread forgotten. Her cheeks flushed. In the theater, she'd grown accustomed to the sight of men without their shirts. The quarters were simply too cramped, the timing too tight to allow for strict modesty. But there was something very different about seeing Quentin's bare chest.

Perhaps it was because his chest seemed so much more muscular than the ones she remembered seeing backstage. Maybe it was that the surroundings were more intimate. Or could it be the fact that she had explored every inch of his chest in the not-too-distant past? Her fingers curled into her palms, remembering the feel of crisp hair against her skin.

"Katie?"

The way he spoke her name reminded her that she was staring at him. She blushed again, dragging her gaze upward, but that was no better. She couldn't meet his eyes without remembering the abandoned way she'd responded to him. She directed her gaze over his shoulder.

"Maybe you should dress. It's a bit chilly," she mumbled.

Since she wasn't looking at him, she missed seeing the amused light in his eyes when he took in her flushed cheeks and the careful way her eyes looked everywhere but in his direction.

"You're right. Now that you mention it, it *is* a bit cool."

Unfortunately for Katie's peace of mind, it took Quentin only a moment to finish dressing. She was still staring at the burned bread when he strode back into the room, his boot heels loud on the wooden floor.

"Don't worry about the bread," he told her, seeing the direction of her gaze. In truth, she wasn't concerned any longer about her latest culinary disaster. But she could hardly tell him that.

"I'm getting used to it," she said, turning to look at him. She called on all her acting skills to keep her tone and expression normal, as if nothing momentous had happened.

Quentin poured himself a cup of coffee from the pot always left warming on the stove. By this late in the afternoon, it resembled thick tar, but Katie had learned that the men liked it that way.

She turned from him, finding it easier to sustain her casual air if she wasn't looking directly at him. She brushed a few crumbs from the table into her palm, wishing he'd say something.

"Are you all right?" She jumped when his voice came from directly behind her. She hadn't heard him move.

"I'm fine." Her voice was too high, her words too fast. She cleared her throat, taking a deep, calming breath. "I'm fine," she repeated, more calmly.

"Then why won't you look at me?" His hands settled on her shoulders, turning her to face him. She stared very hard at the third button on his shirt.

"I've looked at you," she mumbled to his chest.

"Do you truly think I married you out of pity?"

The question brought her eyes to his face as she

remembered the things she'd said when he'd brought her in out of the storm.

"I...I don't know," she admitted at last, her eyes dropping back to his chest. "I don't know why you married me."

Quentin released her, turning away to pick up his cup. "We haven't talked much, have we?" he said, as much to himself as to her. He leaned one hip against the edge of the sink, his eyes on her.

"I married you for just the reasons I gave you in San Francisco. I felt we could build something together. There are those who will tell you that men settled the West but that's not really true. It was the women who brought civilization with them. The women who demanded schools and churches and streets that were safe to walk.

"I've lived here alone for several years and I could feel civilization slipping away from me. A true home needs a woman, children," he added softly.

Katie felt a warm glow inside at the thought of children. His children. Her hand slipped unconsciously to her stomach. Even now, she could be carrying his child. It was an incredible thought.

"I needed someone to help me build this ranch," he went on. "Someone strong. A woman who didn't expect to be waited on hand and foot. A woman who could take care of herself. That's why I married you, because I believed you could do those things."

"You needed a woman who knows about cooking and cleaning and caring for animals," she said, a note of despair in her voice. "I should have told you at the start that I'd no experience with such things. But because you were offering a home, a place to sink roots—'' she shook her head ''—I didn't have the strength of character to tell you you'd made the wrong choice.''

''I went to San Francisco with the idea of bringing back a wife who could stand beside me. I'm not disappointed in my choice. You've done fine, Katie.''

''No, I haven't. You see, I've never kept house or cooked much. We never settled in one place long enough for me to learn.''

''Your family moved often?'' he questioned, realizing that he'd given little thought to her background beyond what he'd seen. He knew her parents were dead but he knew little else.

''We rarely spent more than a few weeks in one place.''

''What did your father do?''

''We were a theater family,'' she said, meeting his eyes directly, her chin raised, as if daring him to think less of her because of it.

''Theater?'' Odd, he'd never have imagined Katie coming from that background. The theater people he'd known had generally been outgoing to a fault. ''*You* were on stage?''

''Yes.''

She waited for his reaction, wondering if he'd find her background embarrassing. Though times were changing, there were still many who felt that being in the theater put one on the lowest possible social rung, barely above that of a scullery maid.

''Why didn't you tell me this before?'' He didn't seem upset or angry, only curious.

''You didn't ask, and I thought I could learn the things I needed to know without your being any the wiser.'' She poked one of the blackened loaves. ''I wanted you to feel you'd made the right choice in marrying me. I know your parents didn't approve. Maybe they were right.''

''No, they weren't.'' He set his cup down and took her by the shoulders again, shaking her gently until she looked up at him. ''I *did* make the right choice when I married you, Katie. I'm glad I married you.

''You've brought warmth and light into this place. You've turned it into a home, just as I knew you would. The cooking and the cleaning aren't important, though you've done a fine job there.''

Katie heard little beyond his first words. He was glad he'd married her. The only thing that would have made her happier was if he'd told her that he loved her.

And who knew, in a world where even flight had been shown to be possible, perhaps love would come, too.

KATIE TOOK UP her pen and wrote,

May 1905
Dear Edith,
It's been too long since I last wrote, I know. I can only tell you that my life has been so full, I seldom have time to draw a breath, let alone write a letter.

I am glad to hear that you and Colin have made peace and that you are seeing him occasionally. I know it's foolish but I do worry about him. He's a grown man, I know, but it makes me feel better to know that he has friends like you.

You mustn't blame Johnny too much for his attitude regarding females working. After all, most men would feel the same. Indeed, many women would feel his position is the correct one.

I agree with you that a century but a few years old deserves to go on without outmoded notions clinging to it from years past. But I think it will be many years before we see changes in the position of women, human nature being what it is. Changes on paper are much easier to make than changes in attitude.

You mention women getting the vote soon, which I found interesting since here in Wyoming, we already have the vote. Indeed, we have had it for nearly forty years. Although I'm sure it's a very good thing and agree that women should have the right to their say, since elections can certainly affect our lives and those of our children, I can't say that my life would be much different if we didn't have suffrage. There's little enough time for worrying about the politicians when I've a house to keep. I suspect it's much the same for other ranch women.

Indeed, between the garden and the chickens and the house, I could make use of several more hours in every day. Quentin has ordered me a sewing machine from the Sears and Roebuck catalog. Nearly twenty dollars it's costing, which seems a great deal of money, but he insisted.

We had a terrible hailstorm nearly two months ago and I thought the garden entirely lost. Fortunately, I've found that plants, no matter how fragile they seem, are quite sturdy, rather like hu-

mans I guess. Most of the plants survived and
they are now thriving.

Life in Wyoming is so different from that in
the city, I'm not sure how to go about describing
it to you. The first and most obvious difference
is the lack of people. Though we have neighbors,
I've yet to meet them, for they live several miles
away. Spring and summer are very busy times on
a ranch, leaving little time for visiting. Quentin
says that there is a harvest dance every year,
which we will be attending in the fall.

I've seen no one but Quentin and the hands
since coming here. I must admit that the solitude
can be somewhat wearing. I miss having a chance
to chat with another woman. It's a lonely life but
a very good one, I think.

I'm afraid my loneliness has made me ramble
on more than I should have and I'm sure you
have better things to do than to read my mean-
derings.

Please let me know how Colin goes on. I've
had only one card from him since leaving the city
and I'm afraid it wasn't very informative. Write
soon.

> Your fond friend,
> Katie.

Katie blotted the last page carefully before setting
it aside. She'd been intending to write to Edith for
weeks now. It seemed as if there was so much to tell,
it was hard to know what to put down.

Of course, the most important news was something
she wasn't quite ready to share with anyone. She set

her hand over her stomach, hardly daring to hope that her suspicion was correct. Carrying Quentin's child would make her life complete, or nearly so.

"You're a fool, Katie, to be always wanting more than you have," she whispered to herself, trying to banish the melancholy that threatened to darken her mood as she folded the letter to Edith and slipped it into an envelope.

She and Quentin had developed a certain closeness over the past two months. It might not be love, or at least not a grand, passionate love, but it was enough for now, or so she'd made herself believe. Love could grow. *That* she did believe.

Katie realized she'd been hearing the odd sound for some minutes before she became consciously aware of it. She stood up, crossing to the door and stepping out onto the porch.

It was a beautiful late-spring day. The yard, which had been a sea of mud for so long, had suddenly sprouted greenery that she thought nearly as beautiful as a finely clipped lawn. The roses she'd planted were showing strong new growth, green leaves as delicate as the life she was nearly sure she carried within her. Before summer's end, she'd be able to step out on the porch and breathe the deep, rich scent of them.

The noise was closer now. It sounded, for all the world, like a motor car, a most unlikely thing so far from town. But that was exactly what came into view. A bright yellow automobile, bouncing and rattling its way down the rutted lane.

People. Katie felt her cheeks flush with excitement, her breath catching in her throat. It had been so long since she'd seen anyone other than Quentin and the hands. She'd hardly know what to say to anyone outside that small circle.

A movement on the other side of the barn caught her eye. Obviously, Quentin had heard their visitors' arrival for he was riding down the hill toward the ranch. Maybe this was one of their neighbors, the ones she'd not expected to meet until fall.

It was her first opportunity to meet the people she'd be living among. She lifted her hands to her hair, suddenly aware that it was in a terrible state of disarray. And the apron she had on was dirty. Turning, she ran into the house, trying to simultaneously straighten her hair and untie her apron.

Her hands were shaking as she settled the hairpins more firmly in the hope that they would hold the unruly mass in place. There was only a moment in which to replace her apron with a crisp white lawn one trimmed with a band of embroidery just above the deep hem.

The sound of the automobile sputtering to a stop in front made her fingers fly as she tied the apron strings. Giving a last pat to her hair, she hurried outside. The car had drawn to a halt in front of the steps. There were two people in it, both so swathed in dusters, goggles and gloves it was difficult to tell anything about them except that one was male and one was female.

"Hello there. You must be the gal Quentin married." The driver was extricating himself from behind the wheel as he spoke. "I'm Angus Campbell and this is my wife Louise. We're pleased to make your acquaintance."

He tugged off his gloves and hat and tossed them into the seat behind him. With only the goggles, he looked rather like an insect and Katie was hard-pressed not to giggle, more from nerves than amusement.

Then his wife spoke. "Take off those silly goggles, you old fool. You look like a bug-eyed monster. Probably scaring the girl out of a year's growth. And come help me out of this contraption. Every bone in my body is shook loose, I swear."

As the man hurried around to help her, Quentin rode into the yard. His horse took instant exception to the bright yellow vehicle, backing and fighting the bit, convinced he was facing something dangerous. Quentin swore, but didn't try to force the pony any nearer. He swung down from the saddle and turned the horse, giving him a swat on the rump that sent him trotting toward the barn.

"I do believe that creature has more sense than this husband of mine," Louise Campbell complained as her feet touched solid ground again.

"Now, Louise, you're the one who said we had to come meet Quentin's bride."

"I don't see why we couldn't have come in the buggy, just like civilized folks," she complained good-naturedly as she shed her driving hat with its veil.

She was something above middle age, Katie guessed, a sturdy woman who seemed very comfortable with who she was and with her place in life. There was warm good humor in her face.

Quentin strode across the yard, gesturing for Katie to come down off the steps as he and Angus shook hands. She moved to his side, feeling as shy as a child at a party. Quentin put his arm about her waist, his pride obvious to their visitors, if not to Katie herself.

"Katie, this is Angus Campbell and his wife, Louise. They're our nearest neighbors, about fifteen miles to the east. This is my wife, Katie."

"Pleased to meet you," Katie said slowly.

"Well, I can tell you that Louise is more than pleased to meet you," Angus said, reaching out to take her hand and shaking it with the same enthusiasm he seemed to show for everything.

"She's been nagging at me ever since we heard Quentin had brought himself home a wife. This is the first chance we've had to get away. I must say, if I'd known how pretty you were, I might have made it a point to get here a little sooner. Pretty as a prairie flower, you are."

"Leave the girl alone, Angus. Can't you see you're embarrassing her." Louise shifted her stocky husband aside, taking Katie's hand more gently, her faded blue eyes kind. "But he is right that I've been anxious to meet you, my dear. There are few enough womenfolk out here. It will be nice having a woman so close."

"I'm very pleased to meet you. I was beginning to think no one else lived in Wyoming. We haven't had any visitors."

"Well, you'll have a few this summer. Once the spring work is over, we manage to get in a bit of visiting. Not as much as you're used to in the city, but a bit. Folks out here tend to be pretty friendly. There's few enough of us that we don't get on one another's nerves."

"So, what do you think of her, Quentin?" Both women turned as Angus patted the front of the bright car with the same fondness he might have shown for a child. "She's a Pope-Toledo, made just last year. Got her in Denver for hardly more than a song from a fellow who'd just bought himself a brand new Daimler. Wife said two cars was an extravagance so he sold me this one.

"Had it shipped to Laramie by rail and just picked it up two weeks ago. She's a mighty fine piece of equipment. Mighty fine."

"A song," Louise snorted. "Cost every penny of two thousand dollars and can't do as much as a four-bit horse. A toy, that's what it is, Angus Campbell. It's a toy."

Angus was not visibly dashed by her scolding tone. "She won't admit to it but she enjoys it almost as much as I do. I've been trying to talk her into taking a trip in it, maybe all the way across the country. Couple of fellas did it two years ago in a Packard. New York to San Francisco in fifty-two days."

"It looks like a fine automobile, Angus," Quentin said, circling the vehicle slowly. "But it doesn't seem very practical. If it gets stuck in mud, you've got to have a horse to pull you out. Seems easier just to take a horse to start with."

"You wait, they'll be the wave of the future. Won't be very long before horses are a thing of the past."

"Maybe in the cities," Quentin agreed. "But I think there'll always be a use for a horse in the country."

"Let's leave the two of them to their talk about that silly machine and go into the house and have a comfortable coze," Louise suggested.

"Will you be staying for supper?" Katie asked as they climbed the steps.

"We'd take it kindly. It's a long trip back and I'd not like to do it on an empty stomach."

Later, when she had time to think about it, Katie was surprised to remember the instant kinship she'd felt with Louise Campbell. Maybe it was the similarity of their situations—both women isolated in a land that seemed more suited to the male of the species. Or maybe it was the warmth that Louise seemed to radiate.

Whatever it was, within a matter of minutes, Katie felt as if she'd known the older woman for years. They worked together comfortably in the kitchen, preparing supper, which was suddenly a festive meal. Louise had brought pies and some of her special chokecherry jelly.

There was so much talk and laughter at the table that it didn't seem as if anyone even noticed the food but the men certainly devoured plenty of it. Some of the talk was about what was happening in the world beyond Laramie.

J. Martin had ridden Agile to victory in the Kentucky Derby. President Roosevelt had visited Colorado only a month before, hunting bear. It was beginning to look as though the Russians had lost their war with Japan. Admiral Togo had destroyed their last hopes in the Strait of Tsushima. Now President Roosevelt was trying to negotiate peace between the two nations.

Angus felt that it was best if the United States kept to herself—"No need to go interfering in the rest of the world's business," he said. "If they want to go to hell in a handbasket, that is certainly their privilege."

Quentin argued that, if the United States was going to be a world power as the war with Spain had certainly proven, then certain responsibilities went with it.

But most of the talk centered around the ranch: how the grass looked this year, whether or not next winter was likely to be a bad one. There was only one uncomfortable moment and that was when the talk turned to the ever-present conflict of sheep versus cattle.

"I say we ought to lynch the lot of them," Angus declared angrily. "Damn sheep come in and ruin the range so it's not fit for a jackrabbit to live on. And they stink."

"Cattle are hardly sweetly scented," Quentin said mildly. "And there's a lot of land, enough I suspect for all of us."

"There ain't never been enough land for cattle and sheep to exist side by side. You mark my words, there ain't never going to be enough land. Damn sheepherders ought to be run out of the state before they do more damage."

"Remember what happened a few years ago when Tom Horn tried it, Angus. He got himself hanged for it. Times are changing. The days of cattle ranchers being able to ride roughshod over everyone around them are over. Like it or not, we're going to have to learn to live with the sheepherders."

"Well, I don't like it. I still say, if we'd just all get together, we could run them out, lock, stock and barrel."

"You'd have to count me out of anything like that, Angus." Quentin spoke quietly, but there was an undercurrent of steel in his words. "We don't own this land. All of us are grazing on government land. You can't run people off land that doesn't belong to you.''

There was an uncomfortable silence, which Louise broke by standing up and announcing that it was time for dessert. It didn't take long for the earlier atmosphere to be reestablished, but Katie remembered the scene. She'd been proud of Quentin for stating his case so calmly. She didn't understand the details of the conflict but she had utter confidence that her husband was in the right.

After the meal, the gathering moved outside. Some of the hands started a game of horseshoes and Quentin and Angus were soon pitching the heavy shoes, arguing good-naturedly over the scores. Louise and Katie sat on the porch, Katie with a pair of socks she was knitting for Quentin to occupy her hands and Louise piecing together scraps of fabric to form a quilt square.

''Around harvest time, we usually have a quiltin' bee or two,'' Louise said, her eyes on her work. ''There's a bunch of us and we usually manage to get quite a bit done in amongst the gossip, which is the real reason we get together.''

''I'm afraid I don't know how to quilt,'' Katie admitted.

''Ain't nothing to it. Simplest thing in the world. You just sketch out your design, if you're of a mind to do something fancy. All it takes is a few scraps and an eye for puttin' them together.''

Katie doubted that it was that simple, but she watched the pieces coming together under Louise's fingers and decided it was something she could teach herself, what with her stitching skills. It would be nice

to have a quilt she'd made herself for their bed. And
for the child she was nearly sure she carried.

"I tell you, Quentin, that horse is a killer." Angus
and Quentin had left the horseshoes to the hands and
spent some time down by the corral. Now they settled
themselves on the shady steps, accepting big glasses
of iced lemonade from their wives.

"There's nothing can be done with a horse like
that," Angus continued. "'Cept shoot him or geld
him, begging your pardon, ladies."

"He's too valuable to do either," Quentin said,
leaning back against a post. "If I can get his blood-
lines into my stock, I'll be able to get top dollar for
his foals."

Katie looked over their heads to the golden stallion
who paced the perimeter of his corral, tossing his head
in their direction as if he knew they were talking about
him. The play of muscles under tawny hide and the
sunlight catching in paler mane and tail made him
seem like an exquisite statue come to life.

"He's not so bad," she said without thinking.
"He's just a little cranky."

"Cranky?" Angus turned to look at her, his shaggy
brows almost meeting his hairline. "That horse darn
near took my arm off the one time I tried to ride him.
That's why I sold him to Quentin, here. I'm not going
to have a vicious animal on the place."

"He's not vicious," Katie said firmly. "He just
needs attention."

"The only attention that animal needs is a bullet
between the eyes," Angus muttered before taking a
deep swallow of his lemonade.

"I don't quite agree with Angus," Quentin said,

turning to look at Katie. "But don't go getting the idea in your head that Laredo is just misunderstood. Some animals are rogues and there's nothing that can be done to change that. You give him a wide berth, Katie. If you offer him a sugar cube, he's likely to take your hand along with it."

Katie shrugged, turning her attention back to her knitting. It gave her a pleasant feeling to hear Quentin sounding concerned over her safety. She could hardly spoil the moment by telling him that she'd already reached an understanding with the big horse.

There were so many days when she thought she'd surely go mad if she didn't have someone to talk to and the stallion had proved an undemanding audience. She could lean on the top rail of the corral fence and say anything that came to mind.

At first, he'd stayed on the other side of the corral, watching her warily, convinced this was some human trick to get a rope around his neck. But when nothing happened, he'd eventually gone back to his business.

Katie had started setting sugar cubes on top of the rail, feeling that if he had to listen to her rambling, he deserved a reward. It had been nearly a week before he'd come take the sugar while she was still there, but he'd finally decided she wasn't dangerous.

She'd yet to touch him but she didn't doubt that the day would come when he'd let her lay her hand on that beautiful neck of his. Time enough to tell Quentin then. In the meantime she just basked in the concern he was showing. It made her feel almost loved.

Chapter Ten

June 1905

Dear Katie,

I know I should have written before now for I have important news for you. But before I get to that, I want to tell you how much I've enjoyed your letters.

I graduated from Mrs. Lutmiller's Academy of Typewriting and Essential Office Skills only last month and have been able to put my diploma to use. I am employed in a secretarial capacity by the manager of Stevenson's Emporium. I find I enjoy the work very much, certainly a great deal more than working at the Sterlings'.

They, by the way, had a terrible fight with old Mr. MacNamara. I'm not quite sure of the details but it seems that Mr. Sterling had suggested that he might forbid your Quentin to enter the house again.

Mr. MacNamara, on hearing this, hit the dinner table with his fist and said that, as long as his money was supporting the household, he would be the one to decide who would be welcome and who would not be.

I had this information from Mary, who was serving dinner that night, for I had already left their employ for reasons I shall tell you presently.

Anyway, Mr. MacNamara said that he felt Quentin had made a fine choice in marrying you and that you were both welcome in *his* house any time you cared to visit. Mrs. Sterling fainted and had to be carried up to her room, though Mary told me privately that she believes Mrs. Sterling to have softened her attitude and thinks she would welcome the two of you.

With that out of the way, perhaps I should tell you my news, which involves my reason for leaving the Sterling household even before I had received my diploma.

I know you will be surprised to hear that I have wed. You will recall that I had on several occasions spoken slightingly of the institution of marriage and hinted that it was not for me. How the mighty are fallen, I confess.

But perhaps the biggest surprise of all will be when I tell you whom I have married. I know I had mentioned to you previously that I have seen your brother on several occasions.

Only a few weeks ago, he took me to the Chutes, where we saw Mr. Charles Rigney perform his high dive, saw a reenactment of the Johnstown Flood and rode in the Circle Swing. It was quite an exciting night for me, though perhaps not as thrilling to you, since you are more familiar with things theatrical than I.

What all this is leading up to, as you can perhaps guess, is that Colin and I are wed. Only a week past, we went to Oakland, which some are saying is the Gretna Green of California and were married. My parents had forbid the match, not approving of Colin's employment at the Rearing Stallion.

Once the deed was done and they saw how happy I am, they forgave us and welcomed him into the family. The next day, Colin found employment at the Grand Opera House on Mission Street. He said that he would not be dictated to, but he, naturally, did not wish to cause his new in-laws any concern. I believe it amused my father greatly.

You are perhaps shocked that I should still be employed, now that I am a married lady like yourself. I will be honest and admit that Colin would rather I did not work, but I have talked him 'round by pointing out that my income will help us to put aside money for a little house, such as we both long to have.

I must use my maiden name, of course, and remove my wedding ring before arriving at the office, for I am certain they would never employ a married woman, feeling it unseemly for a female in such a position to hold employment outside the house.

I am very happy to be your sister in marriage, Katie dear. And I hope you will forgive us our unseemly haste. I'm sure you know that, once your brother's mind is decided, he sees no reason to hesitate before taking action.

He asks me to send you his affection and best wishes and the hope that we will all be together again soon.

Yours,
Edith

Katie folded the letter slowly and slipped it back into the envelope. She was hardly surprised by Edith's news. She'd almost expected it. Each letter had contained some mention of Colin. And even in the one letter her uncommunicative brother had written, he'd mentioned Edith.

As she often did when she had something to think out, she found her footsteps leading her in the direction of the corral. Laredo studied her a moment before walking over to the fence where she stood.

"Hello. You want your sugar, do you?" Katie dug in the pocket of her apron and set the sugar on the fence next to her. She'd not yet ventured to feed him directly from her hand, though she thought it was safe enough to do so. She stroked his neck while he crunched the treat between his teeth, snuffling at the rail to see if he'd missed any tidbits. She laughed softly.

"Greedy." He turned to look at her, eyes wary, but he didn't move away.

Colin married. She was happy for him. And for Edith, but the news made her feel slightly melancholy, too. They'd married for love. With little money, only dreams for prospects, they'd married for the most foolish reason of all. How she envied them that.

She sighed, her hand stilling on the stallion's neck. It wasn't that she regretted her marriage to Quentin.

He was all that was good and kind. But she sometimes felt as if there were a wall built around him, a wall he wouldn't let her cross to get any closer.

"Maybe when he lost his Alice, he truly lost his heart. Maybe he'll never love again." Laredo ducked his head as if in agreement and then trotted off.

Katie stared at him without seeing. Could she bear it if Quentin was never more than the slightly affectionate companion he was now? The only place she felt as if he truly belonged to her was in the privacy of their bed. There, she felt no ghosts, no walls. But there had to be more to a marriage than that.

Quentin had said he wanted to build something good and fine. Well, she wanted that, too. But part of what she wanted to build was a strong bond between them, one that would survive any challenge they might face. And she couldn't do that alone. Her palm flattened against her stomach.

Would the child she was now sure she carried provide her with the means to forge that bond? Surely, he couldn't keep her at a distance while she was carrying his child, perhaps a son to carry on his dream.

"You haven't been getting too close to that devil, have you?"

She jumped, spinning around so quickly she had to clutch at the fence to keep her balance. She'd been so absorbed in her thoughts, she hadn't even heard Quentin ride into the yard. He sat on the bay pony just a few feet away, lean and relaxed in the saddle.

"What are you doing here in the middle of the day?" she questioned, surprise making her voice breathless.

"We found a bunch of cattle in one of the canyons.

There's some calves among them who managed to avoid the spring branding. I didn't think they needed me.'' He nodded to where the golden stallion paced at the far side of the corral, eyeing Quentin with deep suspicion. ''You haven't been getting too close to that horse, have you?''

Katie glanced over her shoulder as if she didn't know which horse he might be talking about.

''I've kept a safe distance,'' she said, choosing her words carefully, knowing that his idea of a safe distance and hers might be somewhat different.

''What are you doing down here, anyway?'' Quentin swung his leg over the saddle and slid to the ground, leaving the pony ground-hitched as he crossed the short distance between them and leaned on the rail next to her.

''I come down and talk to Laredo, sometimes,'' she admitted, feeling rather foolish. ''He's more interesting than the chickens, and the milk cow is holding a grudge for my clumsy attempts at learning to milk.''

Quentin laughed, the lines around his eyes deepening in a way that made her long to kiss them.

''So old Bessie holds a grudge, does she? Well, it doesn't surprise me. She always did strike me as a cranky old thing. Does Laredo say much when you talk to him?'' He turned to rest his arms on the top rail, eyes on the magnificent horse.

''Not much, but he snorts and acts like he knows exactly what I'm talking about. Though I suspect he has little appreciation for the finer points of keeping a house.''

''No, I don't suppose he does.'' Quentin glanced down at her, seeing the wistful tilt of her mouth.

"Are you very lonely, Katie?"

She glanced up, surprised by the question. The real concern she saw in his eyes put a warm glow in her heart.

"Not usually. Sometimes I wish we weren't quite so far from town or neighbors. I do get tired of hearing myself talk. But then I don't answer myself back, either, so I suppose I must be a reasonably good conversationalist."

He laughed again but his expression remained thoughtful. "I don't think I'd ever realized how isolated this life would be for a woman. I suppose I should have spent more time around the home ranch."

"Although I didn't expect parties every night and people dropping in at all hours of day and night, I hadn't expected quite this," she said, her eyes roving the wide emptiness that lay beyond the bulk of the barn. "But I've come to appreciate the beauty of it. And the privacy. Oh, I've privacy aplenty. If I wanted to run out to get a dress off the line wearing only my petticoats, there'd be no one to know or care."

Quentin saw the twinkle in her eye and his mouth widened in a smile. "And do you run to the line in your petticoats, Katie Sterling?"

"I do not. Or at least, I'm not going to admit to it if I do."

He laughed again, feeling peace drift over him, as it always did in Katie's company. There was something about her that made him forget everything but the simple pleasure of her company.

"You know I've shown you little of your home," he said thoughtfully. "At least, little beyond what you can see from the house."

"You've been busy," she said comfortably, enjoying the sunshine on her back and the quiet strength she always seemed to feel when he was near.

"I'm not busy now. How would you like to take a drive?"

"Don't you have things you need to do?" she asked, feeling a stir of excitement.

"Nothing that can't be put off for a few hours." There was a mischievous look in his eyes that she hadn't seen since the day he'd convinced Louis to let them dine at Henri's. It was boyish and quite irresistible.

"I've some cold chicken left from supper and cold potatoes. It wouldn't take long to put together a small luncheon."

"I'll hitch up the buggy."

Feeling like a schoolgirl playing hooky, Katie lifted her skirts to her ankles as she ran toward the house.

AN HOUR LATER, Quentin drew the buggy to a stop deep in a canyon, near where a stream ran, bubbling and dancing over the rocks. Willows bordered the streams, and higher up the canyon's sides was the deeper green of pines and the pale shades of quaking aspens, which Quentin told her would turn gold with the frosts in the fall.

Quentin had chosen a level patch of ground, covered with grass. He cleared an area for a small fire to heat some of the coffee, which Katie had learned was considered a necessity at every meal. The simple meal of cold chicken and potato salad couldn't have tasted better if it had been roast pheasant and champagne.

After the meal, Quentin leaned back on one elbow,

watching sleepily as Katie settled herself on one corner of the blanket and took out her knitting. He tried and failed to remember a time when he'd seen her with her hands idle.

"What are you making?"

"A jacket," Katie answered calmly, her fingers steady on the pale blue wool.

"Are you happy?" She glanced up, surprised by the question. Quentin was looking at her, his eyes serious. She felt her heart swell with love. He might not love her passionately, but he cared.

"Yes," she answered without hesitation. It was the truth. She might not have everything she wanted but it was given to no one to have everything. And she knew, suddenly and without doubt, that if all she ever had was his affection, she could live with that. It was more than many marriages ever had.

He seemed content with her answer. He rolled onto his back, staring up at the cloudless blue sky. "The ranch isn't much yet, but I have plans, Katie. With Laredo's cooperation, we could have one of the finest lines of blood stock in the West. Cattle may always be the heart of the ranch, but horses are always going to be in demand. Good horses. And ours will be the best."

"I know they will. Quentin?" She hesitated, twisting her fingers restlessly in the fine wool she held. "Do you ever think of passing all this on to your children someday?"

"Someday. But I plan on being around a good long while, yet." He settled his head on his laced fingers, his eyes drifting shut.

"Quentin? You do want children, don't you?"

Something in her voice must have caught his attention. He opened his eyes, raising himself on one elbow to look at her. She didn't lift her eyes from the wool she held and he saw that her fingers were trembling ever so slightly.

"Katie? Is it... Are you..."

She lifted her eyes to his, nervousness and excitement warring in their depths. "You'll be a father come the first of next year."

"A child," he said, wonder in his voice. "Are you sure?"

"Yes."

"Katie." He reached out to gather her into his arms, holding her close. "You have made me so happy."

He didn't say anything more, but he didn't have to. She'd seen the look in his eyes and knew that she couldn't have given him any gift that would make him happier.

Maybe this child would serve to draw them closer, to erase the subtle barriers he seemed to hold between them.

January 1906
Dear Edith,
I know it's been nearly a month since I last wrote. I hope you'll forgive me. Winter has closed in on our little home and it's difficult for anyone to get in or out.

Tomorrow, Joe is going to leave. He'll return in the spring but there's no real need to keep all the hands on during the winter months. The work is bitter and cold but there's not as much of it.

Joe has promised to post this letter to you in Laramie.

We spent the holiday season very quietly. Just the hands and us. I was so touched by the gifts all the hands made for me and for the baby to come. There was even a small saddle, though Quentin has promised me he won't try to teach the baby to ride until he can walk.

Quentin's gift to me was a piano, shipped all the way from Chicago and hidden in the barn until Christmas morning. I'll confess I shed some foolish tears over it when I realized it was for me. It seems that tears are so much closer to the surface these days. But Quentin didn't seem to mind.

Indeed, he's been very tolerant of my foolishness these past few months. No woman could ask for a husband to be kinder and more considerate. At times I feel as pampered as a princess.

If the lull in the weather holds long enough, Quentin plans to send for Louise Campbell to come and stay with us until the baby arrives, which should be in only a week or two, though I'm told that babies tend to arrive on their own schedule.

She'll be able to stay in the room Quentin added on this summer—it's a nursery for the baby, but we will put a bed in there for our guest.

Though I told Quentin it wasn't necessary to ask Louise to stay, I will confess to you that I'm relieved at the thought of having her here. I know childbirth is a natural thing and women have been doing it since Adam and Eve, but I must admit to a certain amount of apprehension as my time approaches. It will be nice to have another woman nearby.

It grows late and Quentin has already suggested twice that I need my rest, so I'll say farewell for now. When next I write, I'll be able to tell you about your new nephew or niece.

Write soon and give my love to Colin.

Your fond sister,
Katie

Katie stared out the window at the light snowfall and sighed. It was lucky that Joe had left yesterday. From the look of things, the lull was over and winter was settling in again. They were only a week into the new year, so spring was several long months away.

She shifted in the rocker, pressing a hand to the ache that nagged at the small of her back. Quentin had sent one of the other hands for Louise but they weren't expected to be back here until tomorrow. If the snowfall grew heavier, they might not even try to make the trip.

She sighed again before turning her attention back to the tiny bootee on her knitting needles. She knitted a few more rounds before her gaze drifted to the window again. The snow was lovely, but her eyes were beginning to crave the sight of something green and growing.

Setting aside the bootee, she got up and put another log in the wood stove that kept the cold at bay. Wandering to the window, she stared out longingly. Quentin had warned her about the danger of walking on the deceptively smooth blanket of snow. Thaws early in the season, followed by freezes, had left a layer of ice beneath the powdery white.

A movement down by the corral caught her attention. Laredo was exploring his domain. Maybe she should go down and make sure that the ice had been broken in his water tank. Of course, one of the hands did that every morning. Making sure the animals could get to water was one of their primary tasks during the winter. But they might have forgotten Laredo. After all, they all thought he was vicious.

She was reaching for her coat even as she rationalized her reasons for going out. She hadn't been down to the corral in nearly two weeks. It was harder to sneak in her visits when Quentin was around the home ranch so much. But he was away today and if she didn't get out, even just the few yards to the corral, she was going to scream.

The cold hit her when she stepped out onto the porch. She drew in a deep breath, feeling the chill all the way to her toes. At first, it felt bracing. Halfway to the corral, it began to feel paralyzing and she had a momentary doubt about the wisdom of this small journey. But it would be foolish to turn back now.

She paused at the fence, grateful to have something to hold on to. Laredo approached slowly, though she knew the men had done their best to break up the ice beneath the snow here, not wanting to risk losing a valuable animal to a broken leg.

"Hello, boy."

He snorted, reaching out to take the sugar cube she offered him on her gloved hand. Katie stroked his strong neck, talking to him softly, enjoying the feeling of company. Here, the barn sheltered her from the wind that seemed to cut right through her layers of clothing. It felt almost warm in comparison to more open ground.

After a moment, she edged to the gate and pulled it open wide enough to slip through. She'd long ago discovered that Laredo didn't have any objections to her presence in his corral, though he tended to keep his distance. This time, he followed along behind her as she made her way to the water tank.

The ice had been broken, just as she'd known it would be. But actually checking soothed her conscience. That was, after all, what she'd come out for. She turned, startled to find the stallion right behind her.

"Well, so you're lonely, too, are you?" She scratched his forehead and when he didn't object to that, she moved around and brushed the light snow off his back. His winter coat was shaggy and looked warmer than she felt.

Katie gave him one last pat and turned to make her way across the corral. The footing was surer here and that proved to be her downfall. With the cold nipping at her, she took a step too quickly.

She felt her shoe come down on a patch of ice and felt herself start to fall. She threw out her arms but there was nothing to take hold of, nothing to break her fall. She hit the ground heavily on her back. The shock was such that she lay where she was for a moment, the breath driven from her.

It was driven from her again when she felt pain lance across the mound of her belly. She clutched her hands over the child she carried, fighting the panic that threatened to smother her.

"It's all right," she whispered breathlessly. "It's only natural that he'd be protesting such treatment."

Groaning, she struggled to sit up, finally rolling over and pushing herself to her hands and knees. She rested there for a moment, fighting back tears as another pain stabbed through her belly.

There was a movement nearby and Katie turned her head cautiously to see that Laredo had come over and had lowered his head to nudge her. Was it her imagination or was there understanding in those dark eyes?

"You can help, boy. If you'll just hold still." She reached out cautiously, getting one hand on his neck. As if he understood exactly what she was trying to do, the stallion stood rock-still. Katie used the grip on his neck to balance herself as she crawled slowly to her feet.

She leaned against him for a moment, her forehead pressed to his shoulder as the breath shuddered in and out of her. The pains in her belly had nearly subsided. Or was she simply growing too numb to feel them? Was it colder?

One hand still resting on Laredo's neck, she turned toward the house, sliding her feet along the ground. She was nearly to the fence when she felt her foot slipping again. She grabbed frantically for the stallion's mane but her numbed fingers refused to grasp.

She hit the ground harder this time, her head slamming back to connect with the frozen earth. There was a confused moment of pain and it seemed as if lights flashed before her eyes. She struggled to rise, knowing that to lie here was to die. But there was no strength in her and she fell back, blackness sweeping over her like a thick blanket.

Laredo stood next to the fallen woman, waiting for her to get up. When she didn't move, he nudged her with his nose. But there was no response. Only the mournful whisper of the wind.

He snorted, lifting his head before lowering it to nudge her again. She didn't move, didn't seem to notice the white flakes of snow that drifted over her. Not knowing what else to do, the stallion stood guard over Katie's fallen figure.

But he couldn't protect her from the most dangerous enemy of all—the cold that crept up from the ground and drifted over her in a deadly blanket.

Chapter Eleven

Quentin stomped the worst of the snow off his boots on the back porch, shaking the coating of white off his hat before pushing open the back door and stepping into the warmth of the kitchen. He'd let Lefty take his horse to the barn for him. He didn't like leaving Katie alone, with her so heavy with child and even the small delay to care for his horse was more than he could tolerate.

The rich scent of stew filled the air, making his stomach rumble hungrily. It had been too long since breakfast and he'd spent a good portion of the morning wrestling late calves out of snowdrifts. Late calves were always a problem and few of them would make it through the winter, but he'd do what he could to help the ones who'd made it this far.

Katie wasn't in the kitchen and there was no sign of her in the living room. Quentin walked toward the bedroom quietly, thinking that she might be napping, though she seemed to resent time spent sleeping during the day. But the bedroom was empty as was the nursery and the new bathroom he'd put on only last summer.

His heart seemed to skip a beat. There was no reason for her to have gone outside, but she must have done so. Maybe she'd just stepped out front to check the blankets she'd layered over those roses that seemed so precious to her.

He practically threw the front door open but the stoop was empty. His hand clenched over the edge of the door. He shouldn't have left her, not even for a few hours. Where was she?

A shout near the barn brought his eyes slashing in that direction. Lefty lifted his arm in a wide wave, the urgency in the gesture visible even at this distance. Quentin took the steps in one stride and covered the distance to the corral at a pace far in excess of anything that could be called safe.

He skidded to a halt next to Lefty, his heart beating in slow, heavy thuds when he saw what Lefty was pointing out. It could have been nothing more than a bundle of rags, covered with a light dusting of snow, but for the fiery red of Katie's hair spread over the white ground, its color grayed by the snow that had fallen on it.

The big golden stallion stood over her, his eyes on the men at the fence. The scene seemed to tell its own story. He didn't know how or why Katie was in the corral with the stallion, but obviously he'd attacked her. Rage was an ache in his throat, a pain in his temples.

"Get me my gun," Quentin said, his voice as icy as the ground under their feet. "I'll nail that animal's hide to the barn. I swear to God I will."

"Hold on, boss." Lefty set his hand on Quentin's arm. "You can't shoot him. There's too much chance to hurting the missus. 'Sides, there ain't no sign of blood and if he'd laid into her, there'd be more than a sign of it. I seen a stallion stand over a hurt mare like that one time, on guard, like.''

Quentin blinked, trying to clear the haze that anger had put in front of his eyes. Lefty was right. There was no sign of Katie being injured and the stallion didn't look as if he'd just trampled an enemy.

He slipped the gate open, barely hearing Lefty's caution that he be careful. Snow crunched beneath the heels of his boots as he moved toward the fallen woman and the huge stallion.

Laredo watched him warily, dipping his head a time or two as if in warning. Quentin held out his hand, talking soft and low, edging closer to Katie. Laredo trembled but showed no sign of attacking. When Quentin dropped to his knees beside Katie's still form, the stallion dipped his head to nudge her as if to show Quentin that something was wrong.

Quentin stripped off a glove, putting his hand to Katie's throat, feeling his heart start to beat again when he felt the thread of her pulse. He got his hands under her shoulders and knees, climbing to his feet.

Laredo, satisfied that he'd done what he could, snorted and wheeled around, trotting to the other side of the corral, as if relieved to be away from the man smell.

Lefty held the gate for Quentin as he carried Katie out of the corral. He followed him up to the house, opening the front door for Quentin to angle Katie into the warmth.

"Build up the fire," he tossed over his shoulder as he carried her into the bedroom.

He laid her on the bed, stripping his bulky coat off and tossing it impatiently into a corner before going to work on Katie's clothes. She moaned as he lifted her to ease her out of her coat. His hands felt thick and clumsy as he tried to manipulate the buttons on the front of her dress but he managed them at last, lifting her out of the cold garment.

It didn't take him long to divest her of all her clothing. His eyes swept over her anxiously, seeking signs of frostbite. Her skin was pale but not the deadly shade of frostbitten flesh. He drew a deep breath. She couldn't have been lying out there very long, then.

He was slipping a heavy flannel gown over her head when she stirred again, her lashes fluttering. He directed her hands through the sleeves, dressing her as he would a small child, though the heavy mound of her stomach made it clear she wasn't in that category.

"Quentin." The mumbled name was half a question.

"Hush. You're safe in bed and we'll have you warmed up in no time."

"It was so cold." She opened her eyes wider, coming more fully awake. "I went out to check on Laredo and I fell. I'm sorry. You told me not to go out."

"It's okay. I shouldn't have left you alone."

"I've been making friends with him. You told me not to do that, either." She seemed dazed, not quite focused.

"Don't worry about it. He stood over you like a big guard dog."

"I told you he wasn't vicious," she mumbled. "He just needed someone to talk to. We all need someone to talk to."

"Hush." The last thing he wanted to do was discuss whether or not the horse had been lonely, but he reined in his impatience, his hand soothing on her forehead. "I'm going to get you some broth, something to warm you up."

"Quentin, I—oh!" She half sat up, clutching her stomach, her eyes wide and alert.

"What is it?"

But he knew what it was. Whether it had been the fall or just its own particular schedule, his child had decided to make his or her arrival sooner than expected.

Louise Campbell was supposed to be here. But she couldn't possibly be here before tomorrow, if then. Childbirth was a natural thing. Lots of women had babies without a midwife. Katie would be fine. There was nothing to worry about.

BUT TEN HOURS LATER, it was clear that there was a great deal to worry about. Katie's labor had lasted through the afternoon, with the pains coming closer together just as they should. Quentin held her hand, wiping the dampness from her forehead, feeling his fear rise with every pain that gripped her.

It didn't seem right that it should hurt so much but Katie kept assuring that everything was proceeding normally. Louise had told her what to expect and the pain was nothing compared to the joy of holding her child. But Quentin couldn't shake the feeling of disaster that hovered over him.

He told himself it was only his imagination, that Katie must surely know what was right, but the feeling lingered in the back of his mind.

As the pains grew almost continuous and she grew paler and weaker and still there was no child, he couldn't convince himself any longer that it was just his imagination that something was wrong. She arched, her body twisting with pain. He could see the contraction ripple across her taut belly, feel it in the grip of her hand on his forearm, her nails digging deep into his skin. When the pain faded, she seemed to lapse into a state near to unconsciousness.

Quentin eased himself away from the bed, running his hand through his hair. The room was warm, but not warm enough to account for the sweat that dampened his back. He was scared. More than scared. He was terrified. He didn't have to be a doctor to know that something was wrong. Katie was too pale, too weak.

In the front room, he knew the hands were keeping a vigil. Katie had touched all their lives for the better, making them part of a big family. They'd come to love her.

Just as he did.

The thought slipped in so naturally that it was a moment before the impact hit him. He loved her. My God, how could he have been so blind? He loved Katie. How long had he loved her?

How could he have lied to himself for so long? He'd told himself that he cared for her, that he'd married her for practical reasons. And yes, God help him, he'd even told himself that he'd married her out of compassion.

"Quentin?" Katie's voice rose in a moan and he spun back to the bed. Her hands were knotted in the quilts, her body arched with pain. Quentin dropped to his knees, taking her hand in his, trying to will some of his strength into her suddenly fragile body. As the pain eased, she fell back, her skin as pale as the linen on which she lay.

Quentin brushed the sweat-soaked hair back from her forehead, fear almost choking him. Now that he'd finally realized his feelings, he couldn't lose her. Not again. He couldn't bear that again.

"Katie? Can you hear me?"

His voice seemed very far away. Katie opened her eyes with a great effort, seeing Quentin's face hovering over hers. He looked so pale and worried. She wanted to reassure him, wanted to tell him not to worry. But she was so tired. So very tired. Before she could summon up the energy to say his name, the pain came again.

It seemed even more fierce this time, as if a great fist had grabbed her belly and was squeezing. She cried out, her body writhing as she struggled to escape the pain. She was no longer conscious of the fact that it was a child she was trying to give birth to. All she knew was that some alien creature was tearing her apart, fighting all her efforts to expel it from her body.

She whimpered as the pain eased, leaving her trembling and so weak that even breathing seemed too much of an effort. It took a great effort to lift her eyes in response to Quentin's voice.

"Katie, there's something wrong." He was brushing a cool cloth over her forehead. It felt so good. She wanted to close her eyes and concentrate on the gentle stroking. She wanted to drift away on it. Someplace far away where the pain couldn't find her again. But Quentin was still talking, and he looked so serious.

She frowned, trying to understand what he was saying.

"I think the babe is turned wrong. Katie, do you hear me? I think the baby is breach. He has to be turned."

"The baby." She felt a spurt of fear, her hand fluttering weakly to her stomach. Nothing could happen to her baby. Not now. "The baby."

Quentin caught her hand, his eyes fierce on hers. "Katie, I have to try and turn him. Will you let me try? Do you trust me, Katie?"

For one moment, her mind was crystal clear. She looked up into Quentin's eyes, felt the strength in the hand that held hers.

"With my life," she answered, her voice faint but holding a confidence Quentin only wished he felt. "With my life."

"I'll take care of you," he promised. "Everything will be all right."

But she was already in the grip of another contraction and didn't hear him.

Later, she could remember only two things about the time that followed. Pain, an overwhelming, dominating force that threatened to swallow her completely, leaving nothing but a shell behind. And the sound of Quentin's voice. She couldn't grasp what he was saying but she could hear him talking. It was that sound that she clung to when the pain threatened to grow too great to bear.

The pain peaked to a level of agony almost beyond what her weakened body could stand. Through the pain, she heard Quentin's voice, demanding.

"Push, Katie. We're almost there. Push."

She couldn't push. There was no strength in her. Didn't he know that? But still that voice commanded relentlessly. And suddenly she was pushing with the last ounce of strength in her body. Quentin's hand on her stomach aided her as the baby slid from the birth canal at last.

Katie lay back, panting, light-headed with the sudden surcease of pain. It was several seconds before the silence penetrated her dazed mind. Where was the baby's cry? The reward for all these endless hours of labor? She struggled up on one elbow, blinking to clear her eyes.

The baby lay at the foot of the bed, a tiny form, perfect in every way. A boy, Katie noted with one part of her mind. She had a son. But he was so still and pale, much too pale. Even as the realization came to her, Quentin was bending over the infant, covering the mouth and nose with his own mouth, one hand pressing gently on the tiny chest as he sought to breathe his own life into his son's body.

Katie pressed her fist against her mouth, hardly breathing as she watched Quentin repeat the procedure, once, twice, a third time, coaxing the new lungs to take air. He lifted his head and she caught back a frantic sob, sure that his efforts had been in vain. But as she watched, the narrow chest rose and fell, then rose again. One tiny hand stirred and the baby's mouth opened, letting loose a weak, mewling cry. It was hardly more than a whimper but it was enough to start Katie's heart beating again.

Quentin lifted his eyes to hers, sharing the miracle of the moment, unashamed of the tears that dampened his cheeks. His hands were shaking as he lifted his son, wrapping him in a soft flannel blanket before carrying him to the head of the bed.

"Katie Sterling, I give you our son." There was an odd note of formality in his tone, as if he were speaking some ceremony.

"A son. We have a son."

"A beautiful son," Quentin said softly. But looking at her, he realized she was no longer listening. The effort of the past few hours had caught up with her. She was asleep, her finger still resting against the baby's cheek.

He leaned over to brush the blanket back from the infant's face and his son opened blurry eyes to stare up at him, one hand waving aimlessly. He knew the men would be waiting in the front room, anxious to hear that mother and child were well. He should tell them the news. There were probably half a dozen things he should be doing, but he couldn't seem to draw himself away from the miracle that lay before him.

He drew the rocking chair close to the bed and sat down heavily, his eyes on the bed. He'd get up in a minute. In a minute, he'd start trying to deal with everything that had happened. In just a minute.

Outside, a soft wind kicked the fallen snow into gentle whirls. A full moon shone down out of a cloudless sky, though dawn was not far off. A coyote howled from a nearby hill, seeking a mate. A lost, lonely sound.

In the little house, the hands had heard the baby's cry and drawn their own conclusions. Slapping each other on the back as if they were responsible for the tiny new life in their midst, they trooped through the bitter cold to the bunkhouse, making bets on whether the boss had him a son or a daughter.

Laredo snorted his dislike of this late-night disturbance and moved a little closer to the barn, his eyes on the distant mountains.

Quentin slept, his long body crowded into the rocker he'd bought for Katie's smaller frame. His dreams were full of death. Alice falling through the ice, her wide blue eyes pleading with him to help her. Only suddenly, it wasn't Alice, it was Katie, begging him for help, even as the icy waters dragged at her, pulling her away from him.

He stirred, his brow pleated with agony as he saw his life shattered again and again, first Alice, then Katie. The sequence was repeated over and over until he woke, chilled and shaking, just as dawn was breaking.

IT WAS NEARLY NOON when Louise Campbell and her escort arrived, to be greeted by the news that Katie had had her baby the night before.

When Louise bustled into the bedroom, Katie was propped up against the pillows, her son cradled in her arms. Katie looked up, a smile breaking over her pale features when she saw the other woman.

"Well, I see you didn't wait. Didn't I tell you that babies came on their own schedule?" She strode over to the bed, bending over to admire the sleeping infant. "Well, look at that chin. Just like his daddy's. No wonder he didn't wait for me to get here."

As she spoke, she set her hand against Katie's forehead, nodding with satisfaction when she found no trace of fever.

"You look well, despite having to depend on a man. Lefty tells me there was some problem."

"Did you talk to Quentin?" Katie asked, a touch of anxiety in her eyes.

"Quentin didn't say much beyond pointing me in this direction. Man looks like he was drug through a knothole backward."

"The baby was breech."

"Lordy." Louise sat down in the rocker, finding it only slightly more accommodating than Quentin had. "You Irish can't do anything the simple way. How are you feeling now?"

"Tired. And sore. But I'm all right," Katie dismissed her own suffering with a wave of her hand. Holding her son in her arms made the agony of the day before seem a distant thing. "It's Quentin I'm worried about."

"Quentin? Sounds to me like the man did just fine. Breech." She shook her head wonderingly.

"He was wonderful last night. I'd surely have died if it hadn't been for him. And the baby, too. Quentin breathed life into him or he'd surely have died." She stopped, stroking the pale down on the baby's head, her eyes full of tears.

"Well, then what are you worried about?"

"He looks so pale and stern. And he's hardly spoken to me or looked at the baby. Oh, he's been kind, taking care of me and all, but he doesn't smile."

"The man's had a bit of a shock," Louise told her comfortably, pushing the picture of Quentin's set face from her mind. "You gave him a scare, honey, and men don't take kindly to that. Tends to make them testy, it does. Now, look at that, he's waking up."

Louise leaned forward as the baby stirred in Katie's arms. "You think I could hold him?"

Louise's hands were firm and confident as she took the infant. He blinked up at her, his eyes pale blue and unfocused. "He's going to have eyes just like his daddy's, too. Blue as sin."

"I thought all babies had blue eyes," Katie said sleepily.

"That's true, but I'd be willing to bet that this little one is going to keep his blue eyes. Just look at that chin. He ain't goin' to change his mind about nothin'."

There was no answer from Katie. Looking at her, Louise saw that she'd fallen asleep. Settling the baby more comfortably against her ample bosom, she reached out to pull the blanket up over Katie's shoulders.

"Look at her," she muttered, as much to herself as to the infant she held. "Shadows dark as coal under her eyes and her skin pale as the snow outside. You're lucky you didn't lose your mama, before you even had her."

"How is she?"

Louise turned, startled to find Quentin standing in the doorway. He was looking at Katie, and Louise thought it was a pity that Katie couldn't see him now. If she'd ever seen a man's love in his eyes, this was it.

"She'll do. She'll need some care and feeding up but she'll do."

"She was in so much pain," he said, as much to himself as to her.

"Well, nobody said havin' a baby was an easy

thing. But I'd guess if you was to ask her if she thought it was worth it, she'd tell you it was.

"And don't you go thinkin' this means you have to worry about every baby because it means no such thing. Ain't no reason to think there'd be any problems with the others. Why, I know a woman who's first little one was turned, like to killed his mama. But she went on to have eight more and every one of 'em as normal as day. So don't you get in a lather about that."

"She's so small."

"She's small but she's got good wide hips. She won't have any trouble bearin' you a passel of fine sons and a daughter or two, no doubt."

"We'll see."

Quentin didn't add anything more, but Louise had the uneasy feeling that he'd made up his mind that the little one she held was the last Katie would be carrying. She shook her head over the foolishness of men as he left the room.

"I suspect your mama will have plenty to say about that when she's feelin' better. Men just don't understand these things the way a woman does. The best things in life come along with a certain amount of hurt, whether it's havin' a baby or lovin' someone. You don't get anything for free.

"Your daddy's had a scare, but he'll get over it and I'd bet my best petticoat that in a year or two, they'll be presentin' you with a brother or sister. You mark my words."

BUT WHEN SHE LEFT a week later, Louise wasn't quite so confident. It was nothing she could quite put her finger on, but it did seem as though Quentin was holding himself back in a way that wasn't quite the typical reaction of a man who'd so nearly lost both his wife and child.

She turned in her seat as the wagon moved down the lane. Katie was standing on the porch, wrapped in a heavy coat. Louise lifted her hand and saw Katie return the gesture. Quentin stood behind her, his face cool and impassive.

If it hadn't been for those few moments when she'd seen him watching Katie when he thought no one was observing him, Louise might have been more concerned. There could be no doubting that he loved Katie, loved her deeply.

Well, every man dealt with his fears in his own way. Maybe Quentin just needed some time. She turned back around to face forward. If Katie could just have a little patience, she didn't doubt that they'd be just fine.

KATIE WATCHED the wagon disappear over a slight rise and bit her lip against the urge to call it back. Tears burned behind her eyes but she blinked them back. She wasn't going to cry just because Louise was going home to her own family. She was nearly back on her feet again and there was certainly no reason to keep the other woman here.

"It's time you went back inside." The sound of Quentin's voice behind her intensified the urge to cry. She squeezed her eyes shut, drawing in a deep breath of icy air. Her fingers tightened on the peeled wooden pole that supported the porch roof.

"It feels good to be outside," she offered softly,

opening her eyes to take in the yard. "It looks like a penny postcard, don't you think. All white and pretty."

"It's cold. I don't want you getting a chill."

Katie searched his tone for something more than impersonal concern but could find nothing. He might have been talking to someone he'd just met. There was certainly nothing to indicate that she was his wife, that she'd just borne him a son.

"Just a minute more," she said, blinking rapidly. One tear escaped to slide down her cold cheek, but she didn't move to wipe it away. It didn't matter. Even if she'd been facing him, he wouldn't have noticed. He hadn't looked at her in days.

She was beginning to feel that she didn't exist for him anymore. Oh, he was polite. He spoke to her, he inquired after her health. He watched to make sure she didn't overdo. He couldn't have been kinder or more polite. But there was something impersonal in it, as if she were a guest in his home, someone duty required him to care for. What if he was like this for the rest of their lives?

"I think you've been out long enough," Quentin said, mistaking her shiver for one of chill. She turned, but he picked her up before she could take a step.

"I can walk," she protested, linking her arms about his neck for balance.

"You've been up quite a while. I don't want you to tire yourself."

How could he hold her in his arms like this and still manage to make her feel as if they barely knew each other?

He set her down beside the bed and then helped her

out of the bulky coat, one of his, since he'd decided her own coat wasn't warm enough.

"Louise made some soup before she left. Would you like some?"

"Not right now," Katie said, wanting nothing more than to lie down and have a good cry. A complaining cry from the cradle slowed Quentin's departure. Katie sat on the edge of the bed, watching as he leaned over the cradle to lift his son up.

When he looked at his son, the mask slipped away, exposing the man she'd grown to love. She bit her lip. The baby looked so tiny in his father's hands. Seeing them together never failed to bring back those terrifying moments when Quentin had struggled to breathe life into the baby's lungs.

"If you hadn't been here, he'd not be with us this day," Katie said quietly. Quentin glanced at her and she thought she saw a trace of emotion in his eyes, maybe even warmth.

"Don't think about it. It's over and done with and he's a fine healthy babe."

"We haven't talked about what to name him." It was something she'd thought of before, but this was the first time Quentin had seemed approachable enough to bring the subject up.

"That's true." The baby sucked on his knuckle, growing fussy when it failed to provide him with the nourishment he sought. "I do believe he's hungry," he said, handing the child to her without thinking.

It was only when Katie reached for the buttons at the neck of her nightgown that he realized what feeding an infant entailed. He told himself that he should leave, that he didn't want to stay. Katie didn't look at him, but he saw the flush come up in her cheek as she pulled the gown aside, baring her breast, heavier now with the milk she carried.

The baby turned his head, seeking, his face red and cranky. She lifted her breast slightly, jumping when he found the nipple and latched onto it as if starving.

Quentin lingered, fascinated by the sight of her nursing his child. The ribbon that was supposed to hold her hair had slipped loose so that her hair lay over her shoulders like a fiery cloak. One of the baby's flailing hands discovered the bounty, winding into a fist around several curls. Quentin saw her wince and leaned forward to disentangle his son's tiny hand, letting the boy grasp his finger instead.

"Thank you." Katie looked up at him, smiling shyly. "Have you given much thought to a name?"

"What? Oh, for the baby?" He released his finger, stepping back and drawing a deep breath. "No. No, I haven't. As long as he isn't given my name. I've never cared for the idea of naming a child after their parents. Makes life too confusing."

"I'd thought of Geoffrey Tobias, after my father and your grandfather. Unless you'd prefer to put your grandfather's name first," she suggested, looking up at him questioningly.

"No." He cleared his throat, looking away from her. "Geoffrey is a fine name and my grandfather will be pleased to share his name."

"Then Geoffrey it shall be." She stroked her finger over the soft down that covered the baby's head.

"I have things I should be doing," Quentin said abruptly, and when she glanced up, she saw that the mask was back in place. But it had shifted for a moment, she told herself as she watched him leave. Maybe, given time, it would disappear altogether.

March 1906
Dear Katie,
Colin and I were so relieved to hear that you and your baby are both well. You said only that it was a difficult birth, but gave no details. I hope you have fully recovered by now.

You will be pleased to hear that we have purchased a small house. My father provided us with a reference and much of the initial monies. Though Colin did not care for the idea of accepting help from his in-laws, I persuaded him that it was for the best. After all, my father considers it a good investment, saying that the value of real estate is sure to go up.

It is a tiny house, sold as an artist's cottage and really no more than that. It is south of Market Street, so we are not on Nob Hill yet. Just five rooms and a bath but the basement is finished. It cost every penny of three thousand dollars. I know you gasp at such a price, dear Katie, but it really is quite a bargain.

Our only fear is that of fire for nearly everything south of Market is built of wood. However, with Dennis Sullivan as Fire Chief, we are safe as can be. He has been talking to those at City Hall about the need for improved precautions in case of fire.

Though my father feels that Mayor Schmitz is hardly better than a thief, surely he will release the funds Mr. Sullivan is asking for. Or so we must hope.

Colin is enjoying his work at the Grand Opera House. In April, Enrico Caruso himself will be performing here. They do say he is the finest tenor in all the world.

Which brings me to my real purpose in writing this letter. Katie dear, do come and see us. Colin is anxious to meet his new nephew, as am I. Our home is small, but it is large enough to supply you with all the comforts you need.

And I am convinced that the cold weather in Wyoming can not be the best thing for either you or the baby. You have told me that spring is a busy time on a ranch, so I know better than to suggest that Mr. Sterling join you. But surely he could spare you for just a few weeks.

There's no need to do more than send us a wire from the train station. We do not stand on formality with family. Just let us know when to pick you up at the station.

I'll say farewell for now, but I hope that soon I will be saying hello.

> Your fond sister,
> Edith

Katie let the hand holding the letter fall to her lap. Outside, the sun shone with unreasonable brightness. The snow lingered in the shadowed places next to buildings but most of the yard was a sea of mud.

She'd listened to the talk around the supper table and knew that more snow was likely, although there was the hope that winter's back was broken. Spring calving was just around the corner and a heavy snow-fall could be disastrous once calving was begun.

She could see that Quentin was concerned, though he didn't say anything. But then, lately, he didn't say much to her beyond what was necessary.

She sighed, leaning her head back against the rocker, looking down at Geoff, who was lying on a thick quilt at her feet. He was gurgling contentedly to himself, seemingly amused by the movement of his own hands in front of his face.

Quentin's withdrawal could be dated to Geoff's birth, but she hadn't been able to find a cause for it. She'd gone over it a hundred times in her mind and there was nothing that could explain his sudden change in attitude.

She was getting more than a little exasperated. He was a good father, spending more time with the baby than she could imagine most men wanting to spend. It was only when it came to his son's mother that he seemed to have nothing to say.

She'd even been driven to asking him if he was upset with her for some reason. He'd seemed genu-inely surprised and assured her that there was nothing wrong.

"But there is something wrong," she told the baby. "We had drawn closer. I know that wasn't my imag-ination. I'd begun to think that he was coming to love me. And suddenly, he changed." She lifted her hands, letting them fall to her lap. "I don't know what hap-pened but I do know that he changed.

"Is it possible he was just being kind to me because I was carrying you?"

Geoff gurgled, waved at a dust mote that floated on a sunbeam above him.

"But that doesn't seem right. He's so reserved. It's as if he doesn't even like me. But I haven't done anything," she protested, more than a little angry.

She picked up Edith's letter, her eyes narrowing in thought. "Maybe I should accept Edith's invitation. Maybe some time apart will be the best thing."

Maybe he'll ask me to stay.

BUT HE DIDN'T ask her to stay. She brought the subject up after she'd put Geoff down for the night. Quentin was seated at the desk in the front room, his pen scratching as he made entries in the ranch books.

"I received a letter from Edith today," she told him.

"That's nice. How are she and Colin doing?"

Quentin didn't lift his head from the ledger and Katie had to consciously relax her fingers on the knitting needles she held, lest the stitches grow too tight.

"They've bought themselves a small house, south of Market Street."

"Good." He seemed to feel that was the end of their conversation.

"Edith has invited me and Geoff to come and stay with them," Katie said, her voice a little too loud.

Quentin's pen hesitated a moment before going on, and Katie found herself hoping that he'd put a blot on the page.

"Do you want to go?" he asked without inflection.

"Well, Geoff should meet his family. And Edith tells me that Caruso will be singing in just a few weeks. It would certainly be wonderful to see him. Geoff will be needing clothes before too long. I could purchase fabric while I was in the city. It's so much nicer than ordering by mail. When you can really see what you're getting, you can really…see what you're getting.''

She trailed off, aware that she sounded like a fool. But he made her so nervous, the way he sat there calmly writing, as if the world wasn't crumbling around her. Didn't he see that something was wrong? What had happened to their talks about the future of the ranch, *their* future?

''Certainly, if you wish to go, I don't see any reason why you shouldn't.''

It wasn't until she heard him say it that Katie realized how much she'd been hoping that he'd tell her he didn't want her to go. Against all logic, she'd thought that the idea of her leaving might make him realize how much he'd miss her.

''It would not be worth making the trip for less than several weeks' stay,'' she said, a hint of challenge in her voice.

''Of course not.'' He set down the pen, turning to give her a vaguely avuncular smile. ''I think it will be a very good thing for you. I know you've missed Colin. Besides, you've been looking a little peaked since Geoff's birth. Some time in the city is probably just what you need.''

Katie kept her eyes on her knitting so that he wouldn't see the tears that threatened. He sounded as if it didn't matter at all to him that she'd be gone. Or the baby for that matter.

''Yes, maybe some time in the city will be good for me,'' she said dully. She stood up, setting aside her wools. ''I think I'll go to bed now.''

"Fine. I've a few more things to do. When would you like to leave? If the weather holds, the roads should be passable by the day after tomorrow. If we start first thing in the morning and keep up a good pace, we should reach Laramie by nightfall. Not like traveling with snow on the roads, like we did last spring."

"I thought it was a lovely trip," she said, staring into the fire. She'd been so full of hope then, so full of dreams for the future.

"Well, this trip will be much quicker, though not much smoother, I'm afraid. You'll have to bundle Geoff up well."

"Yes, I'll do that." She started toward the bedroom, wanting only to bury her face in her pillow and have a good cry.

"Katie." Quentin's voice stopped her in the doorway and she turned, half hoping that he was going to say he'd changed his mind—he didn't want her to go.

"Don't worry about packing a great deal for yourself or the baby. I'll give you a letter of credit and you can draw on my account. Outfit yourself as well as Geoff."

She nodded, not trusting herself to speak. The door closed behind her with deceptive quietness. Once in the room, she stood, fists clenched, slowly reciting the soliloquy from *Hamlet* to herself. Her father had always sworn that it was the best thing he knew for calming nerves, far better than any potion or compound a doctor could offer.

That done, she undressed for bed, slipping her nightgown over her head before moving over to the cradle to check on Geoff. The baby slept soundly, though she knew that might not last the night.

Quentin was sleeping in the room he'd built as a nursery last summer. When she'd gathered up the courage to ask why he hadn't returned to their bedroom, his eyes had shifted away and he'd mumbled something about Geoff waking in the night and it was better that he stay where he was.

It hadn't made much sense, but she'd felt shy about questioning him further. After all, she didn't want to make it seem as if she were too anxious to have him back in her bed, though in truth, she missed the feeling of his lean body next to hers at night.

Crawling between the cold linens, Katie felt as if they were no colder than her heart tonight. She didn't know what had happened, how it had come about, but she had to face the fact that whatever affection Quentin might have begun to feel for her had died.

Now what she had to decide was whether or not she could continue in such a sterile marriage.

Chapter Twelve

"Katie!" Edith's cry turned several heads besides Katie's. Hitching Geoff further up on her hip, Katie turned toward the sound. She saw Colin first and she felt foolish tears start to her eyes. How could she have forgotten how handsome he was, how tall and strong?

"Katie?" Edith darted around a stout woman who was arguing with the porter about the disposal of her luggage. "You look wonderful! And this must be little Geoff. Oh, what a big boy he is. May I hold him?" Since she was already lifting the baby from Katie's arms, it was a somewhat rhetorical question.

Geoff, who generally objected to strangers, stared in fascination at the woman who held him. Later, Katie decided it might have been the enormous hat Edith was wearing, complete with a stuffed bird that bobbed up and down as she nodded. At that moment, it was such a relief to have finally arrived that she wouldn't have cared if Edith had arrived wearing an entire aviary.

"Katie. How are you, lass?" She all but fell into Colin's arms, feeling her tears spill over. When she was a child, she'd firmly believed that there wasn't any problem her big brother couldn't solve. He'd proven himself equal to fixing the doll her father hadn't had time to look at and to mending her knees when their mother was busy running her lines.

He couldn't fix her life for her this time, especially since she wasn't even sure she knew what was wrong. But just feeling his arms around her made her feel safe and protected.

"Here, here," he protested, half laughing. "You're supposed to be glad to see me, not turn into a watering pot." He pried her hands loose from his coat sleeves, tilting her chin up until he could see her face.

"I am glad to see you," she sniffed, giving him a wide smile to prove it. She bent to dig her handkerchief out of her reticule and missed the concerned look he sent over her head to Edith. "It's been such a long trip and I guess I'm more tired than I'd thought. I don't think Geoff is fond of traveling. He was so cranky. It was a good thing Quentin insisted on getting up a private compartment, else I think the other passengers might have asked us to leave."

She mopped the tears from her cheeks and blew her nose before smiling self-consciously. "You'll be thinking I've turned into a silly goose since I left, but I promise you that's not the case. Once I've had some tea and a chance to rest, I'll be my old self."

In a short while, she was comfortably ensconced in a wing chair in what Edith proudly called the parlor, though it was hardly large enough to bear such a grand name. A cup of tea steamed by her elbow and Edith had provided a plate of small biscuits, which she shyly admitted to having made herself.

Colin solemnly warned Katie to have care, her teeth

might suffer if she attempted his wife's cooking. Edith hit his shoulder, blushing and calling him a traitor. He caught her hand, dropping a kiss on its back and promising to break every tooth he had on her biscuits, if only he could be forgiven.

Watching their silly play, Katie felt a wave of melancholy. This was what a marriage could be like. Husband and wife as friends and companions. If she couldn't have that, did she want anything less?

IF COLIN AND EDITH suspected there was more to Katie's visit than a simple desire to see San Francisco again, neither of them said anything. They gave her just what she'd wanted, time to think. The only problem was that thinking couldn't really give her the answers she needed.

When thinking grew too much to bear, she shopped, outfitting Geoff with a wardrobe that would last him for the next year or two, depending on how fast he grew. And for herself, she purchased fabric such as she'd only been able to dream about in the past. It was always a surprise to find that the Sterling name brought her a certain deference even in the finest of stores.

She indulged in only two ready-made gowns, both for specific occasions. The first was a lovely evening gown of pale green satin with a décolletage that made her blush. Colin had purchased tickets for his wife and sister to see the great Caruso, and Katie had no gown suitable for such an event.

The second gown was a soft day dress in palest apricot, with rows of lace around the hem and hundreds of tiny tucks over the bodice. She closed her eyes to the cost, telling herself that she was a Sterling now and, as such, could hardly go about town wearing the outmoded garments that now made up her wardrobe.

But the apricot dress was also for a special occasion. Though Quentin had told her quite specifically that he did not want her to visit his parents, Katie simply couldn't pretend they didn't exist.

So, the day before the opera, she donned the peach gown, dressed Geoff in a fine little suit of navy and white and called for a carriage to take her to the Sterling mansion.

Looking out the window on the ride, she felt her heart begin to beat more heavily as they passed familiar sights. The exquisite homes on the hill with their marble entries and pillared facades were like something out of a dream.

When the carriage drew to a halt, she waited until the driver jumped down to open her door and accepted his hand as if she were accustomed to such niceties every day. When she asked him to wait, he nodded without question, though she knew that a year ago, he'd have demanded to see some money first.

With a sleeping Geoff cradled in her arms, she turned to look down the street, delaying the moment when she'd have to face her in-laws. In the distance, she could see the blue of the bay. It looked so calm and peaceful. She wished she could draw some of that peace into herself.

Lifting her chin, she turned and walked up the brick path, raising her skirt slightly as she climbed the four stairs and stopped in front of the door. She could hear the bell ring somewhere in the house and she felt almost light-headed with nervousness. Maybe Quentin had been right.

But before she could change her mind, the huge door was swinging open. The maid who'd answered the door was no one she recognized.

"Yes, ma'am?" The deferential tone gave Katie courage. She half smiled, thinking that less than a year ago, she would more likely have been told to go around to the back door.

"Mrs. Quentin Sterling to see Mrs. Sterling, please."

She saw the girl's eyes widen and heard her quick intake of breath. She might have come to work here in the last year but it was obvious that she was well caught up on her gossip.

"Oh my." Without another word, she pushed the door shut, leaving Katie standing on the porch. She stared at the blank door, torn between amusement and indignation. It was only a moment before the door was opened again. This time it was Mrs. Dixon who stood on the other side.

The housekeeper looked down her thin nose at the woman and child outside. She made no effort to conceal her disdain.

"Mrs. Sterling is not at home to you," she said coldly. She would have shut the door without another word, but Katie had been prepared for this and she already had her reply ready.

"Then I'd like to see Mr. MacNamara, if you please. I'm sure he'll want to meet his great-grandson."

Mrs. Dixon hesitated and Katie knew what was going through her mind. She longed to shut the door in the intruder's face, to make it clear that she couldn't push her way in. But if she did so and Mr. MacNamara found out about it...

"Come in, please. I'll inform Mr. MacNamara of your arrival."

Katie stepped into the huge marble foyer, her chin held high. She had nothing to be ashamed of. She had every bit as much right to be here as anyone, if not for her own sake, then for the sake of the infant she held. Geoff was a Sterling and she'd not see him shut away from his family if she could prevent it.

Mrs. Dixon came back down the wide staircase, her back as rigid as if she'd swallowed a steel spike.

"Mr. MacNamara will see you now. If you'll come this way."

If the rest of the Sterling family wanted nothing to do with her or her son, Tobias MacNamara didn't share their feelings. In fact, he positively delighted in their presence in his suite of rooms.

Geoff seemed entertained by his great-grandfather and rewarded him by being on his best behavior. No fussing or crying. Instead, Tobias got to see him at his sunny best.

It was only when Geoff began to tire that the old man turned his attention to Katie.

"So, how's that grandson of mine? Why isn't he here with you?"

"Spring is a very busy time at the ranch," Katie said noncommittally.

"Pshaw. The boy could get away if he'd a mind to. Not having problems, are you?" He didn't wait for her to answer, which was just as well because she couldn't think of a thing to say. "He's a good lad but prone to being moody. He thinks too much. That's been his problem all along.

"Take this girl Alice." He nodded with satisfaction when he saw Katie start at the name. "I thought that might be part of the problem. I might have warned you at the start but we hardly knew each other. Not that we know each other all that well now, but this little boy here, he kind of speeds things up."

"I do feel as if I've known you longer than I have," Katie said shyly.

"I do, too. Told Quentin when he came back that he wasn't going to find the kind of wife he needed among those society girls his mother would have paraded under his nose. Find yourself a good, strong girl with character, I told him. I was pleased enough when he told me the two of you were getting married. Hadn't seen a lot of you, but it doesn't take long to see character. And I saw it in you. Strength, too. He made a good choice."

"I'm not sure he'd agree," Katie said in a whisper, twisting her gloves in her hands.

"Well, if it's Alice you're worried about, don't be. Oh, she was a sweet enough child. Pretty as a picture and good-natured, but she and Quentin would never have suited. She was too soft and too gentle. Quentin would have found that out sooner or later."

Katie longed to believe him. But the very intensity of her desire made her wary. When you wanted something to be true, it was easy to blind yourself to the facts. And the fact was that Quentin had said he'd wanted to die, too, when he lost Alice.

Setting aside the tragic Alice, there was still no reason to think he cared for her. Before Geoff was born, she'd begun to think it possible, but he'd changed so since then, grown so cool and distant.

Still, the visit with Tobias made her feel better. Maybe she shouldn't give up so soon. Maybe Quentin had missed her since she'd left. The one short note she'd received since arriving nearly three weeks ago had been completely impersonal but not everyone could put their feelings on paper.

THESE WERE THE THOUGHTS that were running through her head the next night as she lay in bed, staring up at the ceiling. She could find no answers there and she made a determined effort to turn her mind to other things, like the opera they'd seen a few short hours before.

Caruso was truly as great as she'd heard. An article in the *Chronicle* on Sunday had said that Caruso actually would rather be a good cartoonist than the greatest opera singer in the world and had shown some of his cartoons to prove the seriousness of his claim. Katie found it hard to believe that he'd prefer drawing caricatures to singing grand opera, especially when he was reputed to be earning two thousand dollars a performance.

Besides, the magnificence of the voice she'd heard that night made it clear that his destiny lay with opera. Surely, Don José had never been performed more brilliantly. And if Madame Fremstad as Carmen was, as one critic had said, just a bit dutchy, it was a small criticism.

The glitter of the audience had been fitting competition for the splendor of the audience. Colin had told them that nearly one hundred thousand dollars had been taken in for the one performance, with the best seats going for ten dollars each.

It seemed that the crème de la crème of San Francisco society filled the barnlike building, as much to see and be seen as to enjoy the cultural experience of the opera. There were so many dazzling jewels it was hard to notice any one more than the others.

Mrs. James Flood was one of the more restrained, wearing a tiara, a dog collar, shoulder straps and corsage decorations of diamonds and pearls. Edith pointed out the box occupied by Chief of Police Jeremiah Dinan and his wife. Officers ringed the rear of the auditorium, a precaution against a repeat of the riot that had occurred the night before at the Alhambra Theater when the audience had objected to the quality of the performance being offered there.

Colin had managed to get the night off so that he could attend the performance with his wife and sister and Katie thought she'd never seen him look more splendid than he did in his stiff white shirt and black frock coat.

It had been a lovely evening and, for a few hours, she'd nearly forgotten Wyoming, her marriage and Quentin. But now, lying in her quiet bed, there was nothing to distract her and she found herself wondering if he missed her even a fraction as much as she missed him.

Sighing, she turned her face into the pillow, determined to get at least an hour's sleep before Geoff woke her with a demand to be fed. The mantel clock in the parlor was chiming three and Geoff was sure to be awake by six.

Sheer willpower got her to sleep, but it seemed as

if she'd barely closed her eyes when she was awake again. But it was not the sound of her son's cry that made her start up in bed. It was a deep rumbling sound, like the growl of a great animal.

Katie sat up with a start, noting in amazement that the furniture was moving as if in some bizarre dance. The rumbling became a roar as the little house shook. Her first thought was for the baby who lay in his crib near the wall. She jumped out of bed, only to be knocked from her feet as the floor undulated beneath her.

Lying on the floor, she knew the meaning of absolute terror. It was as if the city had been caught up by a giant terrier and was being shaken like a rat.

The shaking stopped and she lunged upward, running to the cradle to snatch Geoff up. She had time for only that before the shaking started again, more fierce this time. Staggering, she grabbed for the bedpost, clutching the baby to her with her free hand.

She watched in horror as the whole side of the house began to shudder and then suddenly the wall broke loose from its moorings, falling outward with a sound that seemed almost minor in comparison to the sounds of shattered masonry and falling brick that were all around.

Above it all, incongruous as a dream, she could hear the bells of Old St. Mary's Church, north of Market, frantically ringing as if announcing the end of the world. At that moment, Katie almost believed that was exactly what she was witnessing.

The shaking stopped with a last sullen rumble. Aside from the bell, it was suddenly silent, the quiet of the tomb. She could only stand there, trembling, holding Geoff close, her mind nearly blank.

From the corner of her eye, she caught a movement. A calendar fluttered on the wall, the lovely girl pictured on it a contrast to the destruction she so obliviously presided over.

Katie took careful note of the date, focusing her mind on that, as if it were of vital importance. Anything to avoid trying to deal with what had happened.

April 18, 1906.

QUENTIN RODE hunch-shouldered and ill-tempered. Why was it that life never worked out as you had it planned? He'd planned to marry Alice and spend his life with her. Then she'd died and he'd sworn never to love again, never to let anyone close enough that her loss could leave him broken and bleeding inside.

And then he'd met Katie.

He'd admired her spirit. He'd found a certain peace when she was near. And he'd told himself that it would be a good thing to marry her. A man shouldn't go through life alone, he should have heirs to follow after, to inherit what he'd built.

He'd thought Katie would make a good wife and she'd not expect him to love her. They were both entering into this marriage with their eyes wide open. There'd be no shattered dreams and broken hearts to come out of this union. He'd provide her with the home she wanted and they'd build a good marriage, based on mutual goals.

It had been a good plan, he told himself irritably. Only that plan hadn't worked, either. He'd made the singular mistake of falling in love with his wife. He loved the way her nose wrinkled when she laughed, the way she frowned while she was cooking, her eyes anxious on whatever pot she was stirring. He loved the way her hair always managed to escape its pins. The way she blushed when he unbuttoned her nightgown. And then how passionately she responded to his touch. He shifted in the saddle, uncomfortable with the direction his thoughts were taking.

When she'd so nearly died having his son, he had no longer been able to pretend that all he felt was fondness. Faced with losing her, he'd had to face his feelings. But he hadn't accepted them, he admitted. He'd fought them tooth and nail.

He didn't *want* to love anyone that much again. He didn't want to be so vulnerable. He didn't want all his happiness tied up in another person. He'd arranged his life so well. How dare she destroy his neat pattern?

He was ashamed to admit that he'd been angry at her, as if it were her fault that he loved her. And then, like a child, he'd decided that he didn't have to love her if he didn't want to. So he'd treated her like a sister or a niece. He'd stayed away from the bed they'd shared. He'd worked long hours so he wouldn't have to spend so much time alone with her.

He'd treated his love for her like an illness that would go away if given a chance to run its course. He'd been a fool, he admitted to himself.

It wasn't until she was gone that he'd learned the true meaning of loneliness. Oh, he'd been lonely after Alice died, but it was nothing compared to what he'd felt once Katie left.

He'd never had a chance to build a life with Alice, never had a chance to store up the little memories that caught him unawares. He'd walk into the kitchen and feel a pang when he didn't see Katie. He'd even felt lonely when he sat on one of her knitting needles, forgotten beneath a cushion.

His temper had gone from bad to worse after her departure. She hadn't even been gone a week when one of the hands threatened to quit. Quentin had reined in his ill temper after that, but Tate had finally taken him aside and, with the familiarity of an old man talking to a young fool, had suggested that he go to San Francisco and bring his wife home.

Quentin had railed all night against the idea. He wouldn't love her. And then he'd gone into the room they'd shared and stared at the bed where they'd made love, the bed where their son had been born. Crossing the room, he'd pushed his boot against the cradle, listening to the quiet rhythm of the rockers against the wood floor.

The house seemed to echo with emptiness. All the heart was gone from it. Standing there in the empty room, Quentin finally admitted to himself that love was something he couldn't dictate, no matter how hard he tried.

If he'd never known Katie, he might have gone through his life content never to love again. But he couldn't pretend she didn't exist and he couldn't pretend she didn't hold his heart in her hands.

"I love you, Katie Aileen Sterling." He spoke the words out loud and wondered if it was his imagination that made the room seem suddenly brighter, warmer.

Now, here he was, almost to Laramie and frozen half to death. He had fresh clothes strapped to the back of the saddle. He was going to catch the first train to

San Francisco and find his wife and tell her just what a fool he'd been. He'd beg her on bended knee if he had to, but he wasn't leaving the city without her.

He'd started well before dawn and hadn't stopped, choosing to chew on a stick of jerked beef while he rode. It was after dark when he rode into Laramie and made his way to the livery stable. He left his horse to be cared for, giving the man an extra two bits to feed the tired animal a ration of oats and rub him down well.

He walked directly to the railway station, though his stomach suggested that stopping to eat might be a good idea. He'd eat on the train, if he was lucky enough to be able to catch one tonight.

"Hello, Bill. You're working late." The stationmaster turned as Quentin leaned in the ticket window.

"Hello, Quentin. Trains don't pay much attention to other folks' schedules. Goin' somewhere?"

"San Francisco, if you've got a train headin' that direction."

"There's one should be comin' through in about three hours. Bringin' relief from Chicago."

"Relief?" Quentin felt a frisson of alarm.

"That's right. You would'na heard yet if you just got into town. There was a big earthquake just this morning. Newspapers are sayin' the city's leveled. No tellin' how many are dead."

"My God." Quentin straightened away from the window. Katie and Geoff were there. And the rest of his family.

"You still want to go?" Bill questioned. "Don't seem much reason unless you're a reporter."

"Yes, I want to go. My family is there."

"Oh, say." Bill's face wrinkled with concern. "I'm sorry about that. I'd forgot you were from the coast." He shifted uncomfortably. "Well, you know how the newspapers always exaggerate. Probably wasn't near as bad as they make it sound. Your wife there?"

"Yes. And our son."

"Say, that's too bad, but I bet when you get there, you'll find them snug as anything. Sure, they'll be fine."

Quentin turned away without answering. Moving to the edge of the platform, he stared toward the west. Katie was there. And Geoff. Everything he loved most in the world. If he hadn't been such a fool... If only he'd told her how he felt, she wouldn't have gone.

Was his stupidity going to cost Katie her life?

THE HOURS immediately following the quake were like a scene from Dante's *Inferno*. Within fifteen minutes, columns of smoke could be seen rising from various parts of the city. Many of the blazes were in the area south of Market where Colin and Edith's little house lay.

The firemen were well trained and responded with an efficiency that couldn't be faulted, but they were hampered at first by the scattered positions of the fires, which forced them to dissipate their efforts over a wide area.

It wasn't long before another and far more serious problem became evident. The water from the hoses slowed to a trickle and then stopped altogether. When the earthquake had lashed the city, the shifting earth had snapped the water mains, leaving the firemen virtually helpless against the advancing blaze.

All of this Katie learned later. In those first few minutes after the tremors, she could only stand in the ruins of her little bedroom, clutching her son to her and offering up a prayer of thanks that they had been saved.

"Katie? Katie, are you all right?" Colin's voice was harsh with fear. She could hear him picking his way through the shambles to her door.

"I'm fine. And the baby's fine." He thrust open her door, his face white, the tension not leaving it until he saw her standing there unharmed. "Is Edith safe?"

"Yes, we're both all right." He seemed unaware of the cut on his forehead, caused by falling plaster. "You'd better put on some clothes. I'll gather what food we have. There's no telling what this day will bring."

"Colin?" He turned back impatiently. "It might be as well if you put some clothing on, yourself."

He glanced down at his bare legs beneath the hem of his nightshirt and an expression that was almost a smile broke the tautness of his features.

It was the only light moment in a grim day. By noon, one square mile of the city lay in ashes and the fires were still raging. Colin had shepherded his small family out into the street, their food tied in a blanket that he carried like a hobo's knapsack. In a matter of hours, it was clear that their little house was doomed. Indeed, the whole area south of Market was doomed.

Without water, Fire Chief Sullivan's brave men could do little to fight the flames. And they later learned that Dennis Sullivan himself had been fatally injured, trying to rescue his wife.

Desperately, the firemen tried to dynamite all that

lay in the fire's pathway, hoping to stem its advance. There was hope for a short time that Market Street's great width might save the area to the north, but the worn wooden building on East Street north of Market soon caught fire.

The fire burned for three and a half days. The great Palace Hotel, which had boasted huge water tanks on its roof to provide its own protection from fires, burned before dusk, its water tanks empty.

As Katie hurried through the streets, seeking safety somewhere beyond the reach of the flames, she saw signs of high comedy and high tragedy. There were men in nightshirts and frock coats, carrying silk top hats and flower vases, whatever had been near to hand when they'd fled their homes.

Several times, they stopped to aid in the rescue of some poor soul trapped in the rubble of a fallen building. Twice, the aid had come too late and Colin had turned away, his face grim, his hands torn and bleeding.

They spent the night crouched in a small park, wrapped in blankets Edith and Katie had carried from their home. Dinner was beans eaten from a tin can and they felt fortunate to have that much.

Katie cradled Geoff to her bosom, wrapping the blanket modestly about her as she nursed, grateful that she didn't have to worry about food for him. Of them all, only the baby seemed to have come through the day unscathed. Colin sat staring at the blazing city below, his arms resting on his updrawn knees, his hands dangling uselessly. Edith huddled against him, her head on his shoulder, her face covered with dirt, except where the tears had wound pathways through the soot and dust.

The sky was bright with the reflected flames. It seemed to Katie as if the whole world was burning. Holding Geoff close, she drew what comfort she could from his sturdy little body. She'd seen enough women, sobbing in the street, begging for some word of their missing children, to know how lucky she was.

Exhaustion finally overcame numbed shock and she lay back, drawing the blanket about her and the baby, closing her eyes and praying that the sun would rise on a better day.

BUT ON THURSDAY MORNING, the fire still blazed. The City Hall, newspaper row and the Grand Opera House where they'd listened to Caruso only two nights before were all gone. The fire was nearing the crest of Nob Hill. Katie spared a thought for the Sterlings, hoping they'd gotten to safety. And old Mr. MacNamara.

Colin moved his small family to the Presidio. Tents and shacks were set up among the rows of military buildings, giving shelter to hundreds of refugees. Military rations were passed out to those in need.

Katie managed to rig a sort of pack that held Geoff to her bosom but left her hands free and she helped out wherever she could, distributing food, bandaging small wounds. She and Edith worked from dawn to dusk, as much to still their thoughts as anything else. Colin had gone back into the city to do what he could. All day, they could hear the sound of blasting as the fire fighters struggled to stop the flames from consuming the entire city.

But it wasn't until midafternoon on Saturday, three

and a half days after the earthquake that the last of the fires were doused. Coal dumps still burned in the industrial area south of Market Street and coffee and tea, stored in a warehouse, continued to smolder, sending out a rich aroma. But there was nothing left near them to burn.

When the news reached Katie, she sat down on the ground and started to cry. For the first time since the earthquake, she allowed the tears to flow. Geoff stirred fussily in his improvised pack and she made a conscious effort to loosen her arms about him. For the first time, she allowed herself to believe that they were going to be safe. They'd be able to go home.

She'd hardly let herself think of home these last terrible days. But it had always been there, in the back of her mind. Something she held close against her fear. Home and Quentin.

Quentin. Was he worried about her? Isolated as the ranch was, it was possible he didn't even know about the earthquake and fire. Had he missed her at all? Or was he relieved that she was gone?

She held Geoff close, laying her cheek against the downy softness of his hair, drawing comfort from his sturdy little body. The smell of smoke was so prevalent she hardly noticed it anymore.

''Colin!'' Edith's voice broke on the cry and Katie looked up in time to see her brother throw his arms about his wife. He was filthy with soot and grime but he was wonderfully, miraculously unharmed. Katie stood up and Colin lifted one arm from Edith's shoulders to draw her close. After a moment she stepped back, reaching up to wipe self-consciously at the tears that had left tracks on her dirty cheeks. Colin, his arms still around Edith, grinned at his sister, his teeth white in contrast to his sooty face.

"I have brought you a present. Someone I happened to run into."

At his gesture Katie turned. Her heart seemed to stop. "Quentin." His name was hardly a breath. He stood right in front of her when she'd thought him a thousand miles away. She blinked, trying to clear the tears from her eyes, sure that she was hallucinating. That wasn't Quentin. She'd thought of him so often these past few days, aching to feel his arms around her. Now that the crisis was past, exhaustion must be making her see things.

"Katie." His voice was low and husky. He was as filthy as everyone else, his work shirt torn, his jeans streaked with soot and dirt. It seemed strange to see him here in the city wearing clothes she'd only seen him wear on the ranch.

She stared at him, searching for something to say. All she wanted was to have him put his arms around her and hold her close, to hear him tell her that he loved her, that he wanted to take her home.

"What are you doing here?" The question was all she could manage.

"I was worried about you and Geoff."

She looked down, stroking her son's hand. Of course he had been worried about Geoff. She'd never had reason to doubt that he loved his child. She blinked back foolish tears.

"Geoff is fine. He's too young to know what's happened. As long as he's warm and fed, he's content."

"That's good." Quentin pushed his hands into his pockets and then pulled them out again, staring at them as if he wasn't quite certain they belonged to him. Around him were sounds of celebration that the fire was at last out.

"Have you been here long?" Katie asked at last.

"Yesterday. I got here yesterday. It wasn't easy. The rails are damaged, you know." He squinted toward the city. "I couldn't find you. Nearly everything south of Market has burned. I'd hoped you and Geoff had gotten out."

"The house was badly damaged by the earthquake," she said, shifting Geoff into a more comfortable position. "Colin got us out Wednesday morning. We've been camping since then."

"So he told me. It was sheer luck that I saw him. I'd still be looking for you otherwise."

"Yes, that was lucky." She stared at his boots, fighting back tears.

"I even went to my family's home."

She glanced up. "Are they all right? We were told that most of Nob Hill had burned. I prayed they got out in time."

"The house is gone. Everyone got out safely. My grandfather commandeered an automobile and packed the whole family across the bay Wednesday night. One of the servants told me they were safe. She also told me you'd been to visit them."

She lifted her chin. "I thought they might want to see their grandson. Your grandfather was most kind."

"But my parents refused to see you." He shook his head, narrowing his eyes against the sun. "My mother was so proud of that big house on the hill, and now the fire has left her with little more than her own servants."

There didn't seem to be anything to add to that. Katie brushed her tangled hair back from her face, knowing that she must look no better than a washerwoman and too tired to care.

Glancing up, she caught Quentin's eyes on her, a look in them she couldn't quite interpret. He looked almost hungry.

"I was coming to see you before I knew about the earthquake, Katie," he said abruptly. "I was coming to take you home, where you belong."

"Quentin?" She felt her heart slow until she could count each beat. She had dreamed of seeing that look in his eyes for so long that she was afraid to believe she was really seeing it now.

"Will you forgive me, Katie? Will you forgive me and come home? It's empty without you. *I'm* empty without you."

There was a frozen moment where she couldn't seem to move and then she was in his arms, feeling them close, strong and warm about her.

"Oh, God, I was such a fool." His voice was muffled in her hair, but she heard the words as clearly as if he'd shouted them. "I love you, Katie. I love you. I thought I'd lost you forever. I couldn't live without you."

She closed her eyes. If this was a dream, then she didn't want to wake up.

Geoff dispelled the dreamlike atmosphere by letting out a loud cry, indignant at the way his parents were squashing him between them. Quentin's arms loosened enough to allow the baby some room. One hand cupped Katie's cheek, his eyes looking deeply into hers. Katie felt fresh tears spring to her eyes at the expression she saw in his.

All her dreams were coming true. San Francisco would be rebuilt, bigger and better than ever. But she wouldn't be there to see it.

She was going to be in a place where you could look for miles without seeing another person, a place where the coyote provided a lullaby at night, a place where she'd put down roots, strong and sturdy.

Leaning her head against Quentin's shoulders, their son held close, she knew she'd found the home she'd always dreamed of and it wasn't really a place. It was right here in Quentin's arms.

Forrester Square

LEGACIES . LIES . LOVE .

He made her a once-in-a-lifetime offer....

TOO GOOD TO REFUSE

by

Mindy Neff

Millie Gallagher's ordinary life is about to take
a fairy-tale turn. Hired as a nanny for Sheikh
Jeffri al-Kareem's young son, she soon finds
herself at odds with her headstrong boss.
To Jeff, Millie is endlessly exasperating—
and equally intoxicating....

Forrester Square...Legacies. Lies. Love.

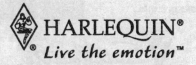

HARLEQUIN®
Live the emotion™

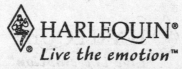

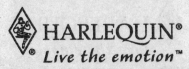